Metaphorosis

November 2023

Beautifully made speculative fiction

Also from Metaphorosis

<u>Metaphorosis Magazine</u>
Metaphorosis: Best of 20xx
Metaphorosis 20xx: The Complete Stories
annual issues, from 2016
Monthly issues

<u>Plant Based Press</u>
Best Vegan Science Fiction & Fantasy
annual issues, 2016-2020

from B. Morris Allen:
Chambers of the Heart: speculative stories
Susurrus
Allenthology: Volume I
Tocsin: and other stories
Start with Stones: collected stories
Metaphorosis: a collection of stories

<u>Verdage</u>
Reading 5X5 x3: Changes
Reading 5X5 x2: Duets
Score: an SFF symphony
Reading 5X5: Readers' Edition
Reading 5X5: Writers' Edition

<u>Vestige</u>
The Nocturnals, by Mariah Montoya

<u>Joyful Heave</u>
Museum Piece: an unusual collection

Metaphorosis

November 2023

edited by
B. Morris Allen

ISSN: 2573-136X (online)
ISBN: 978-1-64076-269-5 (e-book)
ISBN: 978-1-64076-270-1 (paperback)

Metaphorosis
a magazine of speculative fiction
from
Metaphorosis Publishing

Neskowin

November 2023

The Fool Who Sings You to Your Grave

Katie Cervenec

I'm not superhero fodder. The cape, the muscles, the dewy-eyed drive to save the world while sweeping back Ken-doll hair? That's not me. I'm a mediocre Great-Clips visit, brown hair, graying at the temples. I'm a pudge that hangs over my seatbelt, especially when I cram into the jeans I wore years ago in community college.

I've got my window down; it's a warm, windy day in November. My stomach flops when I stop at the next red light and look to my right. Cavill aka 'Cav' sticks his trucker-tanned arm out the window of his red Chevy pickup and gives me the head-bob nod from the second lane over. His eyes literally twinkle when Robert Plant starts up on his radio, singing about that lady and her stairway. I'm surprised it's Led Zeppelin and not Alan Jackson or something with achy-breaky twang.

Over the chug-chug of his idling V8, Cav belts out the words. Holy wailing rock-band, Batman, he cannot sing worth a wet crap. Mouth wide, he looks over at me with eyes that crinkle against the sun's setting light.

They're always light-drenched and full of joy, the ones that listen to old rock songs. I fit my nails to the divots in my Mazda's gray speckled upholstery and force my lips into a tight-lipped smile.

The same song plays on my radio too.

We sing together, terribly, then the light turns green. He gives his head a shake, grinning at me from ear to sunburnt ear. As he rolls away, I hear him whoop out the next verse.

My hands shake.

At the next light, I pull over and hyperventilate in a Rite Aid parking lot, because I saw it all when the song started. I know his name; I read it in the air, but there's more after that. It hovers before my eyes, bolded text, backlit by the lowering sun. An obituary. Tomorrow's.

Cavill Watts Johnston, age 47, died in Sevierville, Tennessee on November 16, 2022.

He is survived by two children, his fiancée and his beloved dog, Callie. He was preceded in death by his parents, Watson and Cherie Johnston, and his sister, Joanne Durnst, née Johnston.

In lieu of flowers, the family requests donations be made to the National Institute for Occupational Safety and Health (NIOSH) Construction Program, or the Golden Retriever Rescue Society.

Three months ago, I called into one of those dumb radio contests. Didn't win. But the static that came over the line right before I hung up? Ear-splitting, stomach-wrenching. Something happened, something wrong.

Ever since, I've been singing radio lullabies with the imminently screwed.

Not sure why this ability attached itself to me; I don't want it. Don't want to talk to or sing with or help anyone; don't want anyone helping me.

I do best on my own.

A tap on the driver-side window pulls my head from the steering wheel.

"Are you okay in there, mister?" a young woman asks.

She's holding tight to the hand of a toddler.

"Just…narrowly missed a fender bender, scared the sh—" I look down at the kid. "Shook me up. I'm fine now."

"Do you need help? Want me to call anyone?"

"No," I answer, more gruffly than I mean to. "I'm fine, great."

Because it's easier than saying I just witnessed a stranger's last earthly moment of joy. It's easier than explaining the truth of my lonely superpower. Every time I hear the same song as a stranger and we sing along together, I know right then, they're going to die that day. *Yeah, I'm great as hell, lady.*

She hurries away. I lean back against the headrest.

At first, I didn't realize what was happening.

There was the couple, just over the state line. I was on my way back from a parts-inspection in Kentucky. I'd stopped at a gas station for a piss and a bag of M&Ms. The couple were in the next parking spot over. White paint all but covered the back windows.

JUST MARRIED
Bryan and Kira 4 EVA
XOXOX
Heart heart heart

An x-rated stick figure drawing someone had tried to smudge off the window.

I grinned.

Four or five Ale-8-One aluminum cans tied to the back bumper.

I was mumbling along to "Brown-Eyed Girl" playing on the radio and casually glanced over. They had started making out, like gophers trying to propagate the frickin' planet. I glued my face to my phone, still bopping with Van Morrison.

I flicked my eyes back up to check up on the crazy kids before backing out of the parking spot. But they were full-grin-

staring at me through the driver's side window. Bryan had a lipstick-stained smirk as he *la tee da-ed* with me. But Kira 4 EVA was belting it out so loud I could hear her voice through the glass. Not half-bad, even at enamored-bride volume. Head back, her natural curls bounced against the top of their car.

We sang the last verse, the three of us, the newlyweds and the stranger. When the song was over, the girl jumped out of the car and ran over. Bryan scratched his head then opened his door. Wiping my melted-chocolate hands on my jeans, I got out too.

There's something about silently sharing music with a stranger. The hush. The inhale. Watching their mouth form the word you're singing. Connection: delicate and cloud-shaped, through two panes of tempered automobile glass.

I asked them where they were from. They asked me where I was going. Kira wiggled on the balls of her Keds-sneakers-with-lace and told me about their honeymoon plan. She wanted to line-dance in a real Nashville bar; he just wanted pancakes somewhere. They both had to be back at work at the factory on

Monday. I gave them five bucks and my congratulations. I meant it.

I live alone. I eat alone; I work alone. But singing with them, I felt connected. Somehow that song tied us together for that moment of humid-Kentucky time.

That first time, there were words, names, burned like an afterimage wavering right outside my windshield, but I didn't pay much attention. Just thought I was tired. When their photos popped up on the evening news — *overturned semi on I65 kills two* — I remembered their names and put my fist through the wall.

After that, there was —

Martina Marie Sanchez-Brumheld, age 34, passed away surrounded by family after a courageous battle with ovarian cancer, in Knoxville, Tennessee... We sang "Despacito" together. She'd glanced out of the passenger window through the rain, drawn and huddled in a fleece pullover and caught me with a thin smirk as I stumbled through the Spanish chorus.

And —

"Happy Birthday" with Ajay Dubois, age 6...

Dammit. I had no idea why that song was playing on my radio, until I turned the corner and saw the wreck.

I held Ajay's hand, 'cause there was no one else left alive by that time. Just a grocery store birthday card playing the same tinny tune sprawled across the broken window, six green balloons in the back of the smashed SUV, and

...happy birthday dear Ajay, Happy Birthday to you

I tried to stop it from happening.

My car radio refused to turn off, so I smashed it. And yet it played. Pried it out and hauled it to a dumpster behind the Burger King. Next morning, there it was, brand-spanking-fracking new in the dash.

I tried working from home so I wouldn't have to drive. Oh, I thought I was onto something then. I wore earplugs when I had to leave the apartment. But do you have any idea how many doctors' offices and stores have Spotify radio playlists turned up to eleven on loop? All it took was one head-bop, one mouthed word and someone was grinning at me.

I used to think it was ridiculous, Batman swooping in on a crime right as it happened; Captain America just hoisting his shield when the bad guys get up to something. But that's how it is: the universe lines us up, puts us in each other's paths, these doomed people and me. It turns out the only thing harder to avoid than a snippet of a melody is a damn flicker of connection, that briefest moment when a stranger and I align our fates for a few notes. And I don't want it.

This morning, I'm taking the bus to a new job. Amazon is always hiring during the holidays. My folks are gone, have been since I was twenty. Not too interested in all the ho-ho-ho and family sing-along stuff, so I won't mind pulling some overtime sorting boxes.

There's a spit-layer of snow on the ground when the bus pulls up and I get on. Next to me, the dreadlocked Black man's headphones start to play the same song that was in my head so loud that I can hear it.

"Let It Go" from Disney's *Frozen*.

Not falling for it, universe, not today. Go pick on some other schmuck.

I forget myself and mouth three words of the chorus. He nudges me and smiles as he sings along in a baritone fit for Broadway.

Before I know it, a single word flashes in front of me, then another, then a line of words, like defiant poem stanzas between the trees and bridges and buildings as the bus chugs along.

Jeffrey Alexander Whitson, age 44, passed away in Catlettsburg, Tennessee on November 23, 2022. Mr. Whitson was earning his culinary degree and spent his free time volunteering at Big Brothers Big Sisters of America. A BBQ dinner will be served for all family and friends in the Springs Baptist Church basement at 4 pm on Saturday following the service.

I ride the bus till he gets off and follow him into a bank, like a lunatic sidekick. It's my first day on the new job. But screw it.

He laughs when I tell him what I know, when I beg him to go home and stay home the rest of the day. "Are you kidding? I've got a girl to propose to tonight."

"You don't understand..." Briefly, I think about asking the bank teller to help me make my case. But what would be the point? No one would believe me; no one will help me save him.

I've got to do this on my own.

The man laughs again. Then he gets mad, because what sort of jackass goes around proclaiming imminent death on a random Tuesday?

When security hauls me outside, I cry. Jeffrey Whitson, the guy who grinned at me on the bus with a mouth full of braces and Elsa-angst is going to die today, and I can't stop it.

I make it to my new job, three hours late, eyes red-rimmed. Mercifully, they're slammed, so they still need me.

I wrack my brain for ideas while I sit through the safety orientation at Amazon. Hell. I'm not going to even open my mouth except to order a Big Mac no onion or to tell off the fruffy politicians spouting their lies on cable TV as I slouch in the comfort of my plaid couch. I just want these strangers to stop dying.

After my shift, my lips sticking together from staying sealed all day, I slink into the suburban library near my apartment. Libraries are quiet. You play a song in there and some owl-eyed librarian will kick the crap out of you.

I like the library.

There's a girl here: Sophia, her name tag says, with blonde hair and skin so pale it's almost translucent. Freckles like a stripe of stars across her nose. I think she's taping barcodes on new books.

I watch her through the half-open workroom door as I pretend to read a fraying Tom Clancy. Holy patriotic good ol'boys, Batman, Clancy loves to hear himself write.

I put it down after about thirty minutes and look at Sophia. Each spine, she aligns with narrow-eyed precision. Each book slots into alphabetical order. All of a sudden, she jumps up, lets out a moaning yell, and her chair crashes to the floor. She shakes her hands in front of her, over and over, over and over.

The librarian sitting at the circulation desk slips into the workroom from the other door. Sophia hits her head with her fist, and I bite my lip. Staying away, keeping quiet is the plan now, but I've got to do something for this woman. My hands shake as I stand up. I pray there's no random song from a phone, or a car blasting its radio outside. I come closer and just stand there. Maybe standing counts as showing up? What the hell do I know?

The librarian, her nametag says Esme, touches her own cheek, then scoots into Sophia's line of sight. Esme's hands move: sign-language. Sophia shakes her head and gives a thumbs-down with the hand that's not striking her head.

I ease into the room, keeping quiet, but Esme, without taking her eyes off Sophia, says, "We're okay. Sophia's deaf, and we're okay. She gets upset sometimes when barcodes get stuck together."

All the while, her hands are moving, talking without words, to Sophia. I toe the rubber base on the wall next to the door. My shoulders relax when Sophia stops hurting herself. She gives a quick thumbs-up and sits cross-legged on the floor, her back now to me.

Esme offers me a small smile then says out loud, "Would you like a drink of water, Sophia?" Her hands move, signing the same words to Sophia, I assume.

I stand there till Esme raises a brow at me.

I'm dense as crap.

In a minute, I'm back with a paper cup of water from the drinking fountain near the bathrooms. I bump into the doorframe, feeling like a praying mantis with too damn many arms and legs.

I place the water cup near Sophia, back up to the door and ask Esme to tell Sophia with her hands that she's doing a great job on the books. I haven't said a word all day; my voice comes out all froggy.

Soon, Esme goes back out front to help a patron. Sophia's still on the floor, so I edge into the workroom again. I slide down the wall and sit so she can see me out of the corner of her eye. She doesn't look at me, but I see her mouth turn up in a small smile. I give her a thumbs-up, open my Tom Clancy again and stay for another hour.

All is calm, all is bright...

I knew this moment would come, didn't know it would be in the library parking lot with a radio Christmas song. It's my day off. Been coming here every few days, when I can. I figured with my new rock-solid commitment to never open my mouth, I could risk driving today. It was just so snowy and cold. I dig into the nailindentions in my car and glance over at the bubble-gum-pink-haired girl with warm brown skin in the VW bug next to me. She's into the song, big-time, even got that Elvis lip-curl going.

Slee-eep in heavenly peace.
Silent night, holy night…

Her pink phone vibrates on the dash and she picks it up, turning down the radio. I fiddle with the dial on my car's stereo, trying to lower the volume. It's playing the same song.

She steals a glance at me, then covers her face, talking into the phone. Whatever it is, it's not good news. It's been longer for me than I'd like to admit, but I know a break-up call when I see one. Poor kid.

My radio chooses that moment to blast full volume.

I see her mascara trailing down to the corners of her mouth. See her mouthed words through both of our rolled-up car windows.

Shepherds quake at the sight
Glories stream from Heaven afar ….

She pauses in the song; my radio's thrumming Elvis's words too.

She points to her dash radio, then motions between her car and mine with a teary smile.

I shake my head pretending I don't know what she's asking even though I know she wants me to sing with her.

"Please?" she says, the word silent in my ears.

Even though I don't understand why, I know it's all up to me. I feel her red-rimmed eyes on me as I turn away without joining in her song. I feel like a monster as I'm saving her life.

On my way home, it starts to snow again. Just windy flurries. That girl, the Christmas Elvis lover. I think I just saved her; I think I did it, and all on my own. When I get to my apartment's parking lot, I get out into the cold night air and stare at the streetlight. Flakes fly like mini-tornados, only visible in the cone of the light. I grin, 'cause it's kind of beautiful in a clunky suburban way. Then, the snowflakes smash together like magnets. They form words.

Cassidy Vinnie, 19, died December 2, 2022 in Knoxville, Tennessee. She was born February 28, 2003 in Augusta, Georgia. Cassidy is survived by many friends and her paternal grandparents,

Lilly and Gavin Vinnie, who raised her. A memorial service will be held Wednesday, December 7th at Victor Ashe Park. Donations may be sent to The Trevor Project, website included below.

I lock myself in my apartment. Forget the new job. Forget the library. Forget Sophia with the stars on her face, though I have to admit that'll be harder to do. I'll never leave again. The image of Cassidy's pink hair burns in my mind when I'm awake, when I try to sleep.

When I finally leave the apartment, days later, I pretend I'm going to get the icy hell out of Dodge, make a beeline for someplace where no one listens to music, wherever that is. But those words in the snow already know where I'm going, and I do too.

I drive to Victor Ashe Park in Knoxville, smashing the pedal to the floorboards. I don't know what I hope to find. Her grandpa sitting on a park bench? A place to sign my condolences in a mild-colored notebook with the Target barcode still adhered to the back?

A shock of bubble-gum-pink hair among the maple trunks?

I don't know how long it takes for the last notes of a soul to flee on still air. I don't know where a person's melody goes. Does it trip over itself like the highest-octave keys or is it more of a *Five-Finger Death Punch* throw-down-type-thing at the end?

Even if I couldn't save her, I've decided to believe that Cassidy's song — her soul — goes somewhere. Somewhere calm and bright.

I rush among the leaf-less trees and trails. At the edge of a small pond, I see a deflated balloon and a wilted bunch of sunflowers. Her name on a program, her picture with that hair, pink as hope.

The service is over, but Death has time to wait.

I feel dumb as shit, but I queue up Elvis's Christmas album on my phone.

Looking out towards the muddy pond, I sing Cassidy every damn word of that damn song.

It's cold.

The wind cuts through my t-shirt and whispers to me what I know, what I've probably always known: I can't stop it.

If I wave my hands and shout, they don't listen. If I follow them, they think I'm crazy. If I don't sing... they still die. I thought it was up to me, but I'm helpless. Stuck in this loop of melodies and words signaling the end of someone's life. It's not me killing them, but they keep dying anyway.

The next day, I sit in the library with Sophia again for four hours. I don't read. We don't talk.

The day after, I go again. And the next.

After about a week, Esme brings me a stack of books, not a Tom Clancy among them. A couple of thin Scholastic copies of Shakespeare plays, one fracking-thick Shakespeare anthology, and a book on American Sign Language.

"You got the wrong guy if you think I want to read all of—"

"Sophia set them aside for you," Esme interrupts.

Sophia scratches her nose.

I find my spot on the floor and open the sign language book.

It's Tuesday, two days before New Year's Eve. I've got no job, nowhere to be. The library and its silence haven't let me down yet, so I join Sophia in the workroom. She expects me now; that feels good. Sometimes I tell her about the book I'm reading. I hope, someday, in her own way, she'll tell me a thing or two as well.

Today she's standing at the end of the table, trucking away at her barcodes as usual. I sit down, still clutching that same Tom Clancy, but I'm bumbling through *The Tempest* now too, on good days. Not today.

"I'm sad all the time," I tell her. It feels strange to really talk to someone, but I'm tired of going it alone.

She watches the words leave my mouth. I know she knows what I'm saying; it's just, words don't mean the same things to her as they do to some other people. I kind of like that.

My story comes out, a few words at a time, in between the paragraphs I read silently to myself about Jack Ryan saving the world.

"I thought not singing with them would save them, but it doesn't work like that. Instead I stole something from her, from Cassidy Vinnie age 19."

Sophia's hands move over the books and barcodes. She stacks one book to the side every now and again. But her eyes stay on my mouth. She's listening, but I can tell it's hard for her. I need to dig deeper into that sign language book.

I mash my palms to my eyes. "Singing with someone, it's fun. Just a little zing of connection in this shit-assed world."

With that, I clamp my mouth shut. She's never going to believe my story anyway; why did I get carried away talking to her like that? We usually just share silence together. I scratch my head and find my place in the book again.

Sophia stacks two more books to the side.

She puts a barcode on a children's board book, but it's a little crooked.

She looks at me and bites her lip; her hands make fists and rise into the air.

I lean back in my plastic chair, stretch my arms out and give her the biggest smile I can find, then I yawn. *This ain't no big thing, Sophia,* I try to tell her with my body language.

Her shoulders relax, her fists unclench.

She gets back to work.

"You're a damn cool cat," I tell her. "Would you like some water?"

She nods.

I hear someone humming to themselves as I walk back. I don't know the song, but I rush away anyway.

I can't stop them from dying. I'm no savior. I'm just the fool who'll sing you to your grave; I'm just one last smile before death's final kiss.

After I place the cup in front of Sophia, I raise my fingers in a *W* at my chin and sign water. And it's probably hokey to hope she wants to spend time with me as much as I want to spend my time with her, but I don't want to miss anything she has to say, no matter how she says it.

She looks up at me and rubs those freckles on her face again. And we stare at each other. Worlds and oceans of sentences, thoughts, songs — I can see them behind her eyes. I stare a moment longer and a dumb thought pops into my head. I could get used to this. Me and Sophia. If I can't sing with her —

She shakes her head, almost violently. I'm convinced she can read my thoughts on my face. She pats the floor where she has spread out a handful of books. My knees creak as I crouch on the library carpet.

She points at the books, left to right, one at a time and gives me a look I can't understand.

I shrug.

Sophia makes a noise, and her fists clench. She grabs my hand, makes my pointer finger stick out.

Like the beats of a song, she moves my finger over the pages. Different place each page, down the line of books, ending on the hardback cover of The Book Thief.

I'm so lost; I want to understand. I just don't. This is on me Sophia, I don't get it.

She does it again. Again. Each time, she lands my finger on Thief, the final note of her song.

Same places each time.

Oh. I'm dumb as shit.

"The … robbed that … smiles, steals … something from… the … thief," I say, reading her words, her song, to me.

"Shakespeare's *Othello*." Esme has peeked her head around the corner of the workroom. She's putting on her coat. "I haven't come by a Shakepeare play yet that Sophia doesn't know mostly by heart. We close in 10 minutes."

She taps the doorframe and disappears.

My finger starts to move again, led by Sophia.

Not Thief.

She punches my own finger into my knee.

Not Thief.

She's telling me it's not my fault. Not my job. I'm not a superhero; I don't have to be.

"All those people, they were going to die anyway," I say. It hurts, but it feels true. It isn't a job I have to do right. It's a gift, a gift I was given to give back to them in the face of death. Connection, light as a cloud, as invisible as a tune, soft as freckles across pale cheeks.

Thought I had to do this all alone. Turns out, I was the one who needed saving. I feel like Sophia knew that all along.

She smiles.

"You're right, Sophia. I got to smile at that thief Death for as long as I can."

I'd be lying if I said I wasn't choked up.

On the way home, my radio starts up. Three ascending horn notes. *Do-dodo*, that 60's beat. A Domino's delivery woman pulls up beside me in a Toyota Camry, with that illuminated blue and red beacon on top. Neil Diamond starts singing about that girl, "Sweet Caroline".

I'm already crying again. But I nod my head to the beat anyway.

Our windows are rolled up, but the delivery driver turns her head to me, already singing along. When she sees my mouth forming the same words, I watch her say "No way. No way!" and then we're singing together again. I don't even know her name. Not yet.

I'm just the musical finale number, big hands, big dance, the last hoorah. The last smile.

So I make it a good one and smile in spite of that thief. Picturing Sophia's grin helps. And she was right; joy floods me. It almost makes me giddy.

We're hamming it up at the red light. The delivery woman smacks her palm against the window, and I lunge over the center console to tap my fingertips to the passenger side window. Neil's singing about hands, touching hands.

We're pointing at each other, pointing at ourselves. My vision is a sea of red swimming brake lights. She's crying now too. It's just a moment so silly, so dumb.

So full. Worth every note. Worth the smile in the face of Death.

I sing to her, and she sings to me.

Sweet Caroline, bum bum bum....

The light turns green. I wipe my wet eyes and look to the road.

A pair of headlights, blinding my eyes, blinding my brain, speeds straight towards me. Crunching metal drowns out the sounds of Neil Diamond. And for a moment, I'm confused. The universe messed up, got the wrong guy. I've just figured things out. I'm not the villain, certainly not the hero, just the singing fool.

The air freshener tag on my rearview mirror flies off, thumps me in the shoulder. I get a strong whiff of pine and then watch it land in the empty passenger seat beside me.

And then I understand. That woman wasn't hearing the same song as me.

I think of Sophia, her barcodes, her banner of stars. She showed me I don't have to be the hero. I'm just an ordinary guy living his life.

Ordinary people die every day.

Neil Diamond and the Domino's delivery woman, sending me out, full of joy and a song.

I heard the same song she did. And I sang along.

See Katie Cervenec's story "The Fool Who Sings You To Your Grave" online at Metaphorosis.
If you liked it, leave a comment. Authors love that!
Remember to subscribe to our e-mail updates so you'll know when new stories are posted.

About the story

I think writing is an intensely personal and soul-baring activity. I wrote "The Fool Who Sings You To Your Grave" when I shallowly felt like the grind of daily life was getting under my skin, but also during a season of hard times in my family where doing the little things felt like a big thing. There's a great sadness in living, and, I believe, there's great hope too. It's all there together. The light, and the dark.

I always like the idea of exploring some very, very ordinary person who suddenly found themselves shouldered with a super-power, which is sometimes just another way of saying — a heavy responsibility. (Which, side note, is kind of all of us.) We'd all love super-human patience, or strength, or persistence, but here we are just doing our best with our ordinary, mortal shells. And the crazy thing is, there's a deep beauty in that.

In "The Fool Who Sings You To Your Grave", the main character, who isn't named, finds himself always singing the same song as the person he's pulled up next to in traffic. And, wouldn't that be fun? What if, while you were belting out Elvis or Beyoncé with the radio, the person in the car next to you was too? I think little moments of connection like that remind us that we're a part of something bigger. But the main character soon finds out his innocuous "superpower" of singing the same song as someone else, has a sinister turn to it. And he's completely helpless against what happens next.

Since I was personally feeling the same about situations I couldn't change, I thought, what can this poor guy do to combat his lack of control? And, like writing often does, it flows answers onto the page that you didn't even realize were there. What do you do? You focus on the small things, the present, the stolen moments of joy. You wring the absolute life out of those times and take hold of the abundance of them. So this is a hopeful story about the beauty of an ordinary someone who shows up, does his best, and sings his song. The rest is out of his hands.

A question for the author

Q: What work of art has been the most inspiring for you?

A: Hands down, the work of art that has inspired me the most is the painting *Mystery and Melancholy of a Street* by Giorgio de Chirico. It's a bizarre, unrealistic painting that has fascinated me ever since art history class in college. There's a term called "chiaroscuro", which sounds stuffy and pretentious, but really just means areas of light and dark in a painting. When I look at this painting, it reminds me that the same holds true for a lot more than just paint colors on a canvas. In writing, in stories, goodness, even life in general, sometimes it's the darkest corners and deepest shadows that make the bright daylight mean more. That's pretty inspiring to me!

About the author

Katie Cervenec is an ear-buds-in writer in the evenings and a commercial interior designer by day. She enjoys sushi, learning about trees, and dabbling in vegetable gardening. She aspires to read 50 books a year but has never quite made it. She's an active member of the Lexington Writers Room and lives in Lexington, Kentucky with her husband and teenage triplets.

katiecervenec.wordpress.com, @ReadKaCerv

It Thaws in Spring

Brittany M. Perkins

Lena lived under the ice. She might have always been there, or perhaps she had lived on the surface once. It didn't matter. Lena could not remember a time when she had not floated in the still waters below the frozen pond, a time when she knew things other than damp and cold and dark.

The under was a vast expanse of water, which, with an effort of great concentration, could be molded into ghostly rooms or objects, though these structures were easily dispersed with a wave of the hand. Impermanence was the way of the under, and it was the way of the ice children as well. There were only four of them now (Lena and Edna and Rebecca and Julian), and every winter began with the uncertainty of how many would remain.

Winter was all Lena knew, all she could experience and remember. She never saw the pond melt in spring, although Edna assured her that it did. Edna never saw this either. Instead, Lena and the others awoke each winter, the ice above them firmly intact, aware that time had passed, but unsure what had happened in the interim. And sometimes, when winter came, someone would be missing.

There had once been more of them, but Lena had not seen Raymond in four winters and Matteo in seven. Lena didn't remember much past twelve winters back, but she had heard other names, of children who had disappeared before her memories began: Cindy, Lola, Isaac. After Raymond hadn't come back, the other children grew more and more distant, until the under became a silent place, and Lena worried that one day he too would be only a name to them.

Lena was drifting through the under, thinking of those who were no longer with them when she spotted Edna, sitting in a chair. A swirling current that had not quite solidified made up its curving frame, and an elaborate tea set was suspended in the space in front of her. Many winters back, before it had become just the four of them, Edna had often talked with Lena, but, lately, Edna rarely acknowledged her at all. Lena approached the girl who had once taught her how to spin up towers and tea sets from the water around them. In the old days, Edna would brighten at Lena's approach and immediately invite her into a story or game she had come up with, but that never happened anymore.

Today, Lena hovered beside Edna, studying her, while the other girl hardly seemed to notice. "Can I join your party?" Lena asked, conjuring a chair of her own, more solid than Edna's, and sitting across from her former friend.

Edna glanced at the teapot and the cup in her hand as though seeing them for the first time.

Lena waited a moment before continuing: "What are you playing? Are you a princess? Or a society lady?"

Edna looked at Lena, opening her mouth as if to speak, but no sound emerged.

"Why don't you talk to me anymore?" Lena asked. "Why don't any of you ever want to play?" Lena rose from her chair, and the structure dispersed into the depths around them. "You used to be fun," she said. And then, softer, "You used to like me."

As Lena withdrew from the girl she had once considered a friend, she thought she heard Edna speak, a barely audible rasp: "I'm sorry."

One of Lena's earliest memories was of Matteo, and it was really more of a feeling than a memory. The memory was a single image of Matteo, pushing a ball made of water toward her. He was laughing. And the feeling was of excitement and joy. That was the best way to describe Matteo: joyful. But the winter before he disappeared, something had been different.

Once, that final winter, Lena had approached the watery rocket ship where Matteo had resided for going on three days. She crept through the half-formed hatch, careful not to disturb the structure's fragile architecture, and inched upward toward the boy who had once filled the underneath with such light and laughter. As Lena neared him, she could see that Matteo was in constant motion, wafting back and forth across the small space at the top of the rocket.

"Matteo?" Lena called up to him.

He did not answer, an eerie smile dragging up the corners of his mouth, as if against their will.

"Are you alright?" she asked. "Do you want to play a game?"

Matteo floated in a slow circle to face her, and although his eyes met hers, they were cloudy and seemed not to see her at all. Then his right hand shot out, grasping for her. Lena couldn't remember what had happened next, but she knew that she had left, and the next thing she could picture in her mind's eye was talking to Raymond.

None of the ice children knew how old they were, but Raymond had always felt older than the rest. So when she told him about Matteo's unresponsiveness, Lena expected an explanation.

Instead, she received a shrug. "That happens sometimes," Raymond said. "Matteo is very social, and it's been hard on him not having new children to play with."

"But I asked him to play, and he wouldn't talk to me," Lena said. "Why does he need someone new if I'm right here?"

Raymond sighed, not meeting Lena's eyes. "I don't know, Lena," he said, the slightest edge of frustration creeping into his voice. "I've tried to tell them—all of them—to be grateful for what we have here, but they always want more. I can't make them happy, and I just..." Raymond clenched his fists so hard and fast that a small current swirled around them. Then he looked at Lena. "You're happy, right? Even with just the six of us?"

"Of course," Lena said, though she wasn't sure that was true. She remembered that feeling of joy from years ago, but she couldn't think of the last time she'd felt it. "I'm very happy, Raymond."

When Matteo didn't come back during the following winter freeze, Lena had been confused. She was the only one who hadn't seen it happen before. Lena had searched for Matteo, and when she was nearly sure but not quite believing that Matteo was gone for good, Lena had asked Edna where he was. She received only a slow shake of the head in response before Edna drifted away, leaving a trail of silt in her wake. Lena soon learned it was taboo to talk about the disappearances, which was why she only had the whispered names of those who had already gone. But Raymond was different. Raymond would talk.

One night, Raymond appeared beside the bed Lena had willed together out of water droplets. The ice children never slept in winter, but they did rest, and sometimes, they dreamed. Lena had been dreaming. In the dream, a girl, whose face Lena could not see, hovered above her, near the ice. Lena was falling away from the girl, as though sucked into an undertow. The girl's hand reached toward Lena, and Lena reached out in return, but their fingers never met. As the distance between the two increased, Lena saw a sunray peek around the girl's head, but she soon faded away, leaving Lena staring into the blaring sunlight.

As Lena tried to call after the girl, she felt algae tickling at the sides of her mouth. She thought it was only part of the dream, until a hand lightly brushed across her shoulder. The coldness of Raymond's skin, which was blue with chill and slightly slimy, like they all were, startled her. Before she could call out, Raymond put a slender finger to his lips. "You want to know what happened, don't you?" He did not wait for Lena to respond. "Do you ever feel alone, Lena?"

Before she could think through the action, Lena nodded.

"We all do, and sometimes we feel so alone that we can't stand it. Sometimes during spring, we get so lonely that our ears are searching, even if we are not. And sometimes our ears find them: the children of the surface. We might hear a laugh or a splash, but it's enough, enough to wake us and call us upward."

Lena's eyes moved back to Raymond's. "Does that mean the others went to the surface?" She sat up, sending loose bubbles and mud flying as her pillow lost form and dispersed. "Is Matteo up there now?"

"We used to have many children," he said. "And for a long time, it wasn't like this. We were happy. We played games. We weren't just... quiet."

"But if they were lonely, why did they leave their friends?" Lena's bed flittered into nothing as she floated upright.

"They were bored with just us," he said. "They needed *new* children—new friends. They got greedy, and now they're all gone."

"Are they on the surface?" Lena's voice was pleading.

"No. We can't live up there. We can't go back, not once we're here."

"Go back?" She thought of the girl from her dream, reaching out to her from the surface.

"More of the surface children used to play on the ice in winter. They would skate and sled, and sometimes, they would fall through. After a while, I guess they decided it was too dangerous."

"What happened... when they fell?" Lena thought she knew, but she didn't want to. She wanted to be wrong. At the edge of her memory, she heard the scrape of blades on ice.

"The ice children would save them. But to save them, we'd have to *change* them, get rid of who they were before. When the surface children stopped coming in the winter, the others still wanted to save them. But that doesn't work in the spring. It only works with the ice. In the spring, they just drown, or they swim away. And if we go after them, we disappear." He took a deep breath, and the water swirled around his mouth. "We're barely here in the spring, not even ghosts, and when we go up there, we're nothing."

"What if we go up in the winter?" Lena asked.

"We don't."

"Why not?"

"Because of the ice." And he turned and drifted away.

Lena was lonely, under the ice. She missed Raymond and his stories about how things used to be. She missed Matteo and his games and high spirits. And it was on a very lonely day, when the sun breached the ice and lit up the underneath, that Lena first heard it: a child of the surface laughing.

Lena soared upward, the water's temperature seeming to rise as she ascended, and stopped just in time not to hit her head on the ice. As she arrived, something thumped above her, and she saw a blurred shadow cover the ice above like a rug. Then the laughter came again, followed by a faint call: "Claire! Claire, get back here. It's too dangerous. Come back to the shore." The caller's voice was like an icepick driving into Lena's brain, and she suddenly felt scared and cold.

"Okay." This voice was closer, clearer, and somehow warmer as well, taking the edge off of Lena's fear. This voice came from the shadow, and as Lena realized this, the shadow moved, became smaller, and began to recede toward the edge of the pond, the water cooling in its wake.

Lena followed the shadow as fast as she could. Claire's shadow quickly outpaced her and was gone, taking the laughter with it. Lena continued her pursuit until she came to the pond's edge. She pressed a hand against it, mud wafting around the point of contact. She tried to grab a chunk of the muddy bank, but it was too tightly packed. Lena let go and wandered back toward the middle of the pond.

When she returned, Lena saw two structures, and she could see the occupants of each through the water that comprised them: a cottage with missing bricks and a crooked chimney (Edna) and a ship that was cracked down the middle, with only half a flag dangling from its too-short mast (Rebecca and Julian). Lena burst into the cottage where Edna sat in a one-armed armchair, a plate balanced on her lap, in front of a fire that would have been roaring had the flames been more than water held in shape by Edna's wishes. When Lena reached her, she stood in front of Edna's chair, blocking her view of the heatless flames. "So, what do you think happened to Raymond?"

Edna choked on her water droplet toast. "What do you mean?" she rasped. Edna looked older than Lena, but not by much. Lena knew Edna remembered longer, though, and knew things the others did not.

"I mean, where is he? And Matteo? Where did they go?"

"It's best not to—" Her voice was clearer now, though still sharp around the edges.

"Raymond said they got lonely and bored and that you think they go to the surface and evaporate."

"Lena."

"I saw someone today."

Edna's eyes brightened for a moment. "Where?"

"She was skating on top of the ice. A surface child." Lena paused, deciding whether or not to go on. "Raymond said there used to be more of us. He said surface children would fall through the ice."

Edna closed her eyes. "Yes," she said. "That was the way. But not anymore." Edna placed a hand on Lena's cheek. "You used to be so warm," she said, and Lena felt a chill run through her, though she wasn't sure if it came from Edna's touch or her words.

Lena recoiled and turned to face the fire, wishing it and its heat were real.

"I wish you still were," Edna said, reaching toward Lena again, her fingers barely brushing Lena's forearm before Lena fled, not wanting that chill to spread elsewhere on her body.

Lena hovered briefly above the cottage, rubbing her cheek. Then she entered the ship, where Rebecca and Julian were clapping their hands together, chanting nonsense rhymes and giggling. The two moved their hands in a circle and spun up three small dolls from the bubbles around them. The dolls hung near Rebecca's head, and she giggled again.

"What are you playing?" Lena asked, moving closer to the pair. "Can I play too?" Lena could remember a time when she had played with the two—Edna called them twins—but that was long ago, when

Matteo and Raymond still occupied the underneath. "When you clap like that," Lena added, still feeling Edna's cold handprint on her cheek, "how does it feel?"

The twins did not look at her. "Did you hear something?" Julian asked Rebecca, not breaking the rhythm of their clapping. Neither seemed to wince or react in the slightest to the other's touch.

"It's the dollies," Rebecca said, inclining her head toward the bubble creations suspended to her left. Lena wanted to reach out and slap one of their hands to answer her own question, but instead, she departed the ship. Once free of the twins' rhymes, Lena willed herself her own structure: a twisting tower, like you would find at the top of a castle, but without the castle.

Lena surged to the top of the tower, which nearly brushed the ice, and as she sometimes had over the past four winters, closed her eyes, and spoke to the only friend who had ever been truly honest with her. "Raymond," Lena said. "I saw someone today. It was a surface child, and she was on top of the ice. I heard her laugh, and I heard someone calling her, and then she got away. I tried to catch her, but she—" A voice seemed to call from somewhere deep within Lena, jerking her sideways and sending pieces of parapet flying. It was the voice that had called Claire, except it was calling for her instead. As Lena shook away the imagined sound, something drew her eyes upward. She looked from the ice to her hands, feeling like they had not always been blue, and almost, but not quite, remembering what warmth felt like. *Claire would be warm.* The thought came, unbidden, and pulled Lena's gaze upward again. Claire would come back. She had to.

After what could have been three weeks or two months—Lena had never been good at measuring time—the light shifted overhead, and Lena felt the slightest kiss of sunlight on her cheek. She flew toward the surface, and, through the icy blur, Lena thought she saw skate blades gliding overhead. She watched for a moment, in awe, and then panic set in. What if this was her only chance to have a friend again? Dizzy at the thought of losing Claire forever, Lena raised a shaking fist and rapped on the ice. In what seemed like an instantaneous response, the figure above collided with the ice with a thud. The shadow filled the patch of ice above Lena, but this time, there was no laughter.

Lena was quick. She pressed her face against the ice to one side of the shadow. Lena rarely ventured this high in the pond, and the solid dryness of the ice always surprised her. "Hello?" she said. "Claire?"

For just a moment, Lena saw blurred eyes in a dark face. Then she heard a muffled scream as the figure jumped up, and the shadow quickly receded toward the shore.

Lena pursued, this time keeping pace for nearly twice as long as before, but still, when the figure reached the shore, Lena could not follow. Lena buried her face in the muddy bank and screamed. As she did, she again heard someone calling her name. It was less of a call and more of a shriek. And then it was all shriek and no words.

The possibility of seeing Claire—she was sure it had been Claire—again filled Lena with such desperation that her stomach ached. The other ice children either ignored her or took from her, but Lena sensed that Claire had something to give, and Lena had not been given anything in a long, long time. Lena thought that if she could talk to Claire, a bit of warmth and joy might make its way into the under, and maybe things could be how they once were. So she hovered under the patch of ice, waiting for Claire's return. She did this every time she could see sunlight, and did not retreat until all light drained away, occasionally scratching or tapping on the ice above to feel closer to Claire and the surface. Lena wondered how many ice children had waited like this. She wondered who had waited for her.

She was engaged in such thoughts when the shadow returned. A soft thud sounded above Lena's head, and she moved as close to the ice as she could.

The blurred face appeared above her. "A-are you still there?" It was Claire's voice.

"Claire?" Lena said, and Claire recoiled. "Wait. Don't. Please."

Claire's face returned. "Sorry," she said. "You're a little bit scary." Claire paused. "Say, how do you know my name?"

Their conversation was muted, as through a tunnel, but Lena could understand her clearly. "I heard someone calling you," Lena said. "The first time I saw you." She paused. "You didn't see me that time."

"Oh," Claire said. "That was my mom." Every word Claire spoke was like a little ray of warmth through the ice, and sometimes, the warmth burned.

The burn at the mention of the screaming woman from their first encounter was too much; Lena needed to change the subject. "Do you like to skate?" Lena asked, and she could almost feel herself gliding smoothly over the ice.

"What? Oh, yes. I do."

These words muted the heat, now more of a comfort than a burn.

Claire continued: "It's just my mom thinks it's dangerous. She doesn't trust the pond to hold out, says I'll fall through."

Lena heard a cracking sound from the corner of her memory and winced again, but it was less intense this time. "Are you afraid?" she asked. "Are you afraid you'll fall?"

Claire laughed, and Lena moved closer. The ice between them made the laugh sound far off, like it was coming from somewhere Lena couldn't quite reach. "No. Nothing scares me. Well, except you." She paused before adding, "But not anymore." Claire's shadow shifted. "Besides, I just come when she's sleeping. Mom sleeps a lot during the day, actually."

Lena didn't know how to respond to any of this. She was overwhelmed and excited and somehow afraid of what Claire might say next.

"I'm sorry. What's your name? I didn't even ask you."

"Lena."

"Huh," Claire said. "My mom had a sister named Lena."

Lena shuddered.

"They used to live where we do now. We moved to the cabin to help when Grandma got sick. She died a few months back."

The feeling of lying under a quilt, safe and warm, filled Lena's mind for a moment until the face of an older girl invaded the vision, scorching it around the edges. "What's your mom's name?" Lena asked, inching closer to the flame of Claire's voice.

Claire's shadow shifted again, and Lena worried that she'd upset her, that maybe she'd leave now. "It's Margaret," she said, finally. "But everyone calls her Maggie."

The name set Lena's thoughts afire. "What... happened... to... her sister?" she asked, needing a break between nearly every word.

"She died. Or they think she did. She must have. They never found a body, though. Mom was a lot older, and she was supposed to have been watching her. Mom and Grandma fought a lot after that." Claire trailed off before asking, "Hey, what *are* you?"

"I—I don't understand."

"Like, how did you get down there? There aren't even fish in this pond anymore. Are you a mermaid or something?"

Raymond had told Lena that there used to be fish. They had disappeared a long time ago, though. Even Raymond hadn't known why. "I'm just down here," Lena said. "I've always been down here. I—I'm an ice child."

"An ice child?" Claire asked. "I've never heard of that." Claire moved her face closer to the ice. "I can't see you very well," she said.

"Not much to see," Lena answered, dragging a fingernail across the underside of the ice and sending a curl of frost receding toward the pond's floor. She didn't want to explain herself anymore. She didn't want to tell Claire about the other children. She just wanted Claire to keep talking, because even though the warmth of her words hurt, they made Lena feel more *real* somehow, and Lena needed that.

"Listen," Claire said, "I have to go. Mom will be up soon, and she'll never let me out of the house again if she knows I've been here."

"Wait—" Lena started. But Claire was already on her feet, skating for shore.

"Do you remember that surface child I told you about?" Lena asked.

Edna was silent, still as the water around her.

"She talked to me, asked how I got down here."

Edna closed her eyes but made no move to speak.

"Was I one of the children who fell? Like they used to? Claire's mother had a sister: Lena."

Edna opened her eyes, pain filling the icy blueness of them. "You were mine," she rasped. "Yes. You fell too. You were skating, but it was too thin." Edna's voice caught a bit. "It shouldn't have been so thin, but it was."

And as she said this, Lena could almost remember. It felt like remembering the feeling of a dream, but not knowing what it was about. "And you saved me."

"Yes. To save one, you have to take out the warmth. They can't live down here with that. But with the warmth goes the memory. Everyone starts over down here."

Lena took a breath. "Did everyone come from the surface? All of us?"

"I think so," Edna said. "I can't know that for sure. I can only remember the ones who came after me, and most of them are gone now. But I remember you, and I remember Rebecca and Julian. They came down together. I remember when Matteo fell. I don't remember a time before Raymond. I think he's the one who saved me. But that was long ago."

Lena still could not remember. Only the shrieking was left, but excitement quickly overtook it. "Maybe Claire will fall," she said.

Edna's eyes brightened. "She might."

"Claire would be new. She could make things good again."

"Would you do that?" Edna asked. "Would you save Claire for us?"

"Of course," Lena said. "I'm tired of alone."

Claire spread out on her belly on the ice. She had not visited in what seemed a long time, and Lena had been antsy. "Sorry," Claire said.

The single word left Lena slightly singed, and she wanted more.

"Mom's been having a hard time. She always does in winter. I think it's—"

"How old are you?" Lena had not spoken to anyone since her conversation with Edna, and her voice came out rushed and clipped.

"Uh, twelve, but I'll be thirteen next month." Claire paused, dragging a gloved finger through the frost covering the ice. "How old are you, Lena?"

"I—I'm not sure..." At the fuzzy edge of something like memory, Lena saw an older girl, someone who loved her and protected her. "Say, how old was your mom's sister when she...?"

"Well, Mom was nineteen, I think, so that would've made her sister eleven."

Lena felt herself swoon slightly, certain now that she was also eleven, and that she had been eleven for a very long time. "Are your friends twelve, too?" she asked a little breathlessly.

Claire sat up, her blurred face blending into the rest of her shadow. "I don't really have any," she said. "They just kind of stopped coming around once my grandma got sick."

"But they could visit," Lena said, nervously scraping the ice with a nail. She imagined how warm they would all be, Claire and her friends. "They could skate with you. You could be friends again."

Claire's shadow shifted slightly. "I don't think so."

"Why not?"

"It just doesn't work like that," Claire said. "We don't talk anymore, and I had to change schools. And Mom doesn't really like visitors. Even before everything... happened, she liked to keep to herself."

Lena was overwhelmed with the feeling of a shy, reserved presence. She sighed, working the edge out of her voice. "That's okay," she said. Then a thought occurred: "We can be friends, then."

Claire shifted again, hesitating. "Th-that's sweet of you."

"You should visit more often." Lena paused, as though deciding something. "It's lonely when you're gone."

"Is it just you down there?"

"Yes," Lena lied. "There used to be others, but they went away."

Claire's shadow was still for a moment. "Lena, did you ever have a sister?"

Lena shrank back from the ice. "No."

"It's just, my mom's sister, she drowned, and I was wondering—"

"It's just me," Lena said. "And I've always been here."

"Listen, I have to get back. Mom will be waking up soon." And before Lena could respond, Claire's shadow began to move away.

When Claire was completely gone, Lena again slid a fingernail along the underside of the ice. Pressing harder this time, she scraped off a thin mist of shavings. Claire didn't understand how important it was for them to be friends, but she would. And so, Lena lingered there, scraping at the barrier between her and the warmth of her new friend until the sun was gone.

That night, just as Lena was nearly to dreaming, Edna appeared at her feet. Lena sat up, dispersing her sleeping mat and waiting for the other to speak, but Edna floated silently, staring down at Lena.

"Edna?" Lena said at last.

"Yes," Edna said, her voice a slowly clearing rasp. "Did you see her today? The girl from the surface?"

"I did."

"And will she be back? Do you think she'll fall?"

"I—I think so," Lena said. "I told her we could be friends."

Edna's eyes widened, a hungry look growing in them. "When will she be back?"

Lena shrugged. "Edna, is it okay to... to *help* them fall?"

Edna's blue-tinged ear twitched. "Do you mean to thin the ice?"

"Uh, yes. I guess so. Would that— would that be bad?"

Edna moved closer, close enough to touch. "We used to do it sometimes, just when we needed more friends. Matteo did it a lot. Raymond was always very mad when we did."

"So, it is bad, then?"

Edna looked away before placing a hand on Lena's forearm.

Lena shivered.

"My hands are colder than yours," Edna said. "Did you know that?"

Lena shook her head.

"You think that we don't talk to you because we don't want to, but really we can't remember how."

"I don't—"

"Raymond said that the other ice children disappeared because they were lonely, that we saved the surface children because we were bored, but that was never it. He didn't understand. You don't either, Lena, because you're the newest, but you will, soon."

Lena retreated slightly, putting distance between herself and Edna.

"I don't remember how to start talking anymore. Someone has to talk to me first, and then I can, but I can't start it. Rebecca and Julian—they were twins before, on the surface, always together— they can only remember how to talk to each other. To save a surface child, we have to take away their warmth, and the longer we're down here, the colder we get."

"And with the warmth goes the memory," Lena said.

Edna nodded. "Yes." She advanced toward Lena. "Do you remember that you used to sing?"

Lena gave her head a single shake.

"You did. All the time, but now it's gone. Sing me something."

Lena tried to think but could not find what singing was. "I can't," she said.

"Because you forgot. And you'll forget more, the colder you get." Edna began to drift back and forth in front of Lena, as though pacing. "Matteo and the others didn't leave because they wanted to bring back children; they left because they were so cold that they forgot they couldn't go. You can't be warm and live down here, and once you're here, you can't go back.

"The reason we saved those children and helped some of them fall was because new children help us remember what it's like to be warm. When the new children stopped coming, we couldn't remember anymore. But Raymond always said it wasn't fair. Not fair. Not fair."

Lena drew her limbs close to herself, as though afraid that Edna would take them from her. "If Raymond saved you," Lena started, "then he'd have to understand."

Edna shook her head. "He was different. Raymond was always different."

"Who saved Raymond?"

Edna shrugged. "We never knew, and he wouldn't say. I think maybe Raymond saved himself. I think maybe he was the first."

"But Raymond left. He must have been cold too."

"Maybe," Edna said. "Or maybe he knew what he was doing. Maybe he didn't want to watch us forget anymore." Edna closed in on Lena again, grabbing her by the collar. "You have to save Claire," she said. "We need her, Lena. You have to save her. I—I'm cold."

And it was true. Lena could feel the chill through her frayed shirt.

"You're the newest, Lena, which means one day you'll be all alone. Alone for real. Things didn't used to be like this. We used to have fun. We used to be happy. You're still warmer than I am, Lena, but touching you is like remembering my name. Touching a surface child would be like remembering who I am. Claire can help all of us."

Lena pulled back, breaking Edna's loose grasp. "Okay," she said. "I'll save her."

"Thank you," Edna said, and she wrapped her arms around Lena tight enough to hurt.

Lena felt a chill run through her, a chill that she was sure would stay there now, for always, although she couldn't remember why.

Whenever the sun broke through the ice, Lena raced toward the surface to wait for Claire, and each time Claire did not arrive, Lena worked at scraping the ice. She would drag her nails back and forth, shaving off the thinnest layers until by the time Claire returned, their patch of ice was noticeably thinner.

Claire arrived this time not in skates, but in boots, and she squatted over the patch rather than lying on her belly. "Sorry, Lena," she said, and her voice sounded hoarse, not quite warm enough to burn just yet, and Lena ached to get closer to her. "Mom's been really bad lately. I think she knows I've been skating on the pond. She won't say anything, but she hid my skates."

As Claire said this, Lena almost felt that it had happened to her instead. Lena had found her skates, though, hadn't she?

"Listen, Lena," Claire started, "I don't think that I'll be able to come back. It's getting late in the season, and Mom's probably right that it's not so safe now."

"No," Lena said. "You have to come back." Lena remembered falling on the ice, someone carrying her, a sprained wrist. She remembered an arm around her shoulder and a kiss on her forehead. "If anything happens, I can save you," she said.

"That's very kind, Lena," Claire said, but her voice did not have the same warmth as her words. "I just don't—Oh no."

"What is it?"

"I think my mom is outside the cabin. I think—"

And then Lena heard it, the screaming woman: "Claire! Claire, come back!" Lena imagined that voice—Maggie—calling her own name, ordering her down from a tree branch or away from a ravine.

"I have to go," Claire said, straightening up.

"No. You can't leave. I have to save you."

The light shifted as Claire turned to go, and Lena pounded her fist against the ice. A sickening crack echoed through the under, and with the crack came a flood of heat. In seconds, Claire was submerged in the water, Lena catching her in her arms. Lena could feel Claire's warmth, and she suddenly had the urge to sing. She knew what singing was now. And then Lena felt a hand tugging at first one leg and then both. Lena looked down into the depths to see Edna's hands around her ankles.

The heat from Claire's body was almost unbearable, but Lena could feel it draining, little by little, and as Claire became colder, Lena began to fill with warmth. She looked at the girl in her arms and saw not Claire but herself, and Edna holding her. Lena remembered the struggle to break through to the surface and the fear as she was pulled down. Someone above was screaming, but that too was fading as Lena descended into the depths, Edna's hands leaching the warmth from her body.

That was when she heard it.

The shriek.

Maggie screamed for Claire, just as she had screamed for Lena back then.

Lena looked at Claire's face and saw her lips beginning to go blue, and she felt the tug of the other ice child at her ankles again.

"Let go," she said, kicking at Edna.

"Save her," Edna rasped.

Save her. She would save her, but not for Edna and the ice children. She would save her for Maggie, Maggie who had always looked out for Lena but still couldn't save her all those years ago.

Lena closed her eyes and kicked against the water. Edna fell away, and Lena felt the light and warmth of the surface. And then she felt air and snow-covered ice. She thrust Claire's body onto the ice and pulled herself out. Lena could feel every part of her wanting to float away, as though she, like most everything else in the world beneath the ice, were formed from fragile water droplets. She willed herself together and scooped Claire into her arms. Lena began to sing. She couldn't remember learning the song, but still, she knew every word: "Oh my darling, oh my darling…"

Lena walked. She pointed herself in the direction of the shore, and she moved.

"Oh my darling, Clementine..." Lena felt her feet begin to fade away and saw that her hands were losing color and shape, but she willed her arms to stay together, just for a bit longer. "You were lost and—" she could see the woman on the shore, frozen to the spot like she had lost her own warmth as well "—gone forever."

What was left of Lena's feet stepped onto the shore. "Dreadful sorry..."

"Claire," the woman breathed, interrupting Lena's song. Then she followed the arms holding her daughter. "Lena?"

"Maggie," Lena said. And as her legs and arms and face dispersed, she remembered all of it.

See Brittany M. Perkins's story "It Thaws in Spring" online at Metaphorosis.
If you liked it, leave a comment. Authors love that!
Remember to subscribe to our e-mail updates so you'll know when new stories are posted.

About the story

I wanted to write a story that takes place in a 'secondary world', and the first line of the story popped into my head: 'Lena lived under the ice.' I didn't know what it meant or what the story would be, but I loved the image and the alliterative nature of the line. Shortly after coming up with the opening line, I went to visit my boyfriend. It was on the car ride to his house that I started internally 'writing' the story. I came up with the scenario, the characters, and even some of the language I planned to use. This was back in November 2022, and at the time, my boyfriend and I would do something we called 'co-work', where we would both work on projects we needed or wanted to get done while keeping each other company. During this visit, we co-worked, and that's when I wrote it. I wrote almost the entire first draft of the story in one sitting, on my boyfriend's couch, while occasionally scratching his Labrador behind the ears. It's evolved quite a bit since then, of course, and I expanded on it a lot during the following months, but that was how the original came about, and it's ended up being one of my favorite things I've ever written.

A question for the author

Q: Q: Do you ever feel bad for what you put your characters through?

A: Honestly, yes. I was the type of kid (and somewhat embarrassingly am the type of adult) who worried about hurting a hairbrush's feelings by not using it enough or throwing it out. So, obviously, I feel bad when I have to bring harm or hardship to a character I've created. When I was younger, this aversion to harming my own creations led me to avoid unpleasant fates for my characters, even if that was what would best serve the story. As I've gotten older and have matured as both a reader and a writer, I can accept that sometimes a character has to suffer for the good of the story. While this may not have been what Stephen King meant when he advised us to "kill your darlings," I think it holds true in this context as well.

About the author

Brittany M. Perkins resides in not quite a small town but definitely not a big city in the Southern United States with her three well-behaved cats and one horribly-behaved cat. Since childhood, she has had the habit of disappearing into imaginary worlds. As an adult, she has yet to outgrow the habit of playing pretend. While she enjoys writing in many genres, she has a penchant for all things speculative.

Rosalind Dreams of Aersea

Travis Burnham

Rosalind was eleven when she got her first hammer, an 8-ounce, Estwing ball-peen. She thought it was the most beautiful thing she'd ever seen, though her Dad had frowned the whole time she unwrapped it. Rosalind's father's first disappointment had been that Rosalind wasn't a boy—he was a carpenter who'd dreamed of a son to follow in his manly footsteps. Rosalind couldn't remember a time when she hadn't wanted to be a carpenter—to be a builder, a maker of places people could call home.

When she was thirteen, she ran the third leg of the 400m relay at the State

Track Meet. Second only to carpentry, she loved running—the warm burn in her muscles and the feel of air brushing against her skin. And she loved the companionship, telling wild stories to her teammates, the shared training and hard work. The team was depending on her points for the meet. On the starting line, her toes were tingling—she thought it must be nerves. But at three hundred meters, her left foot went numb to the ankle and she stumbled to the track surface. Scraped and bleeding, she pulled herself up and hobbled across the finish line. It would have been easier to bear if her teammates or coach had been angry.

That night, she had her first seizure, opening a gash in her forehead on the way down to the yellow kitchen linoleum. Nearly the only thing she recalled of the experience was the gentle voice of her older stepsister, Muriel, trying to talk her through it. When, five weeks later, Rosalind was diagnosed with Taeka-Storovski Syndrome, she was told she'd be lucky to make it to her 17th birthday.

This was Rosalind's father's second disappointment—and he didn't stick around for a third. Rosalind's mother stayed, but was never quite the same after. She'd always been somewhat mousy, and the abandonment drained something vital from her, making it seem like everything she did was just going through the motions.

As Taeka-Storovski dismantled Rosalind's body, she raged against fate. She cried, she screamed into her pillow, she shattered plates in the kitchen and smashed her favorite 'Dark Side of the Moon' record. One morning, she woke to her throat still raw and her vision bleary from crying the night before. She could barely feel her right hand. Down in the kitchen, she poured some milk into her Lucky Charms with her shaky offhand and looked over the room with exhaustion. Her eyes fell upon the fold at the top of the milk carton: SELL BY 10/26/23. This milk would go bad in five days. Her eyes fell back to her soon-to-be-soggy cereal as she realized she, too, had an expiration date, and would most likely be dead in three years, maybe less.

She didn't want to spend her remaining days in complaint and misery. She would try hard to be grateful—the disease was destroying her ability to do many things, but it left her imagination intact. She had always told stories to her teammates, or invented tales for herself about strangers she saw, but what if she were more ambitious? That night, she began constructing an entire world she'd call Aersea in her mind.

Aersea began as a single, floating stone. Rosalind perched on it with her beloved ball-peen hammer—which she knew was not the best tool for the job—to pound and chip the floating boulder into shape. Made of cloudstone, the stone was a white, porous mineral, flecked with mica and lighter than air. When she needed it, another chunk of cloudstone would appear. Rock by rock, stone by stone, boulder by boulder, amid oceans of clouds, the archipelago of Aersea came together. She was a carpenter of worlds.

The construction of Aersea wasn't flawless. Sometimes the wrong stone would appear, a piece of dense granite or quartz or marble, and it would fall, shrinking into the unknowable distance. Sometimes, she would swing the hammer wrong and a piece of cloudstone would shear off and spin away. She'd hew a forest from cloudstone and breathe life into it, imagining it as verdant green, but as life flowed into it, the leaves would resolve to mother-of-pearl, and the bark become noctilucent.

As Aersea grew, she'd gaze out over what she'd created. And it was then she'd notice geographical features she *hadn't* created—a range of low slung hills, an achingly clear lake filled with cloud-white trout, a forest of cloud firs festooned in white needles.

By that time, Muriel had been offered a dream job working for *Destinations*, a travel website with a monthly magazine. She didn't want to accept it, as she knew it would take her away from Rosalind. Their mother and the nurses were good caretakers, but they couldn't be big sisters.

The night before Muriel had to make the decision on the job, she was stretched out in bed with Rosalind and they were staring at the glow-in-the-dark stars on the ceiling. "I don't want to leave you, Rosie." The quiet gasping of the respirator was a constant background noise. Rosalind depended on it more and more of late. Being on the respirator was terrible, like she was constantly drowning. But it was even worse without it—like running the 100m with a pillow strapped to her face.

Rosalind took a deep, raspy breath and said, "I need you to see the world for me, Murzie. Please." The more of Aersea she built, the more Rosalind realized she was going to see none of her own world. Rosalind would miss Muriel terribly, really couldn't imagine what she would do without her, but even worse was the thought of both of them losing their dreams. She buried all the selfish thoughts that would keep Muriel home.

From the pillow next to her, Rosalind took a tattered, pink, stuffed bunny and tucked it into the crook of Muriel's arm. "You can take Energizer with you. It will be like I'm there, too."

Muriel turned away for a moment, blinking back tears. Rosalind offering the bunny was a gut punch—a reminder that her little sister was just a little kid dealing with much more than she should have had to: dying with dignity.

In the end, Rosalind begged for Muriel to take the job, and Muriel relented.

Muriel sent letters and postcards to Rosalind. She texted photo upon photo upon photo of herself and Energizer—from the altiplano of Colombia, with the little stuffed bunny wearing hiking boots and riding on Muriel's shoulders, or of the stuffed bunny perched on the walls of Monsaraz Castle, looking out over the lake-spattered plains of the Portuguese Alentejo. Yet another of Energizer wearing swimming goggles and being held above the Klein-blue waters of Rota in the Mariana Islands. One postcard from the Marianas read:

> *We dove with sea turtles! Okay, Energizer saw them from the dive boat, but still! I'll bring back loads of dive pictures to show you. My love for you is deeper than the Mariana Trench!* ♥ *Murzie*

Many of the landscapes Muriel described would find their way into Aersea.

Time flowed differently there. Rosalind would doze off and a day would go by among the clouds—but when she woke and looked at the clock, only an hour had passed.

But the creating was becoming harder. More and more things she hadn't created herself began appearing. It seemed the worst injustice that she was losing control in both worlds. She did her best to reframe the losses in a positive light.

Small towns dotted the landscape. She thought of the movie *Field of Dreams* that her dad had made her watch when she was eleven—the main character kept hearing a voice telling him that if he made it, they'd come, or something like that. There were people living in Aersea. Had she given them a place to live? It had always been her ultimate goal as a carpenter—to provide shelter.

When Muriel wasn't working or traveling, she was home with Rosalind. Muriel was never negative—she didn't want to waste any of her precious time with Rosalind with complaints. They'd talk far into those nights, reminiscing. Muriel told tales of her travels—the Great Wall, the Great Barrier Reef, the Great Ocean Road—and Rosalind about the changes happening in Aersea, where she was spending more and more time. Muriel was fascinated with the depth of detail Rosalind had for her imaginary Aersea.

"Do you remember when we made war clubs that winter?" Rosalind asked. "And then smashed sheets of ice down on the Merrimac?"

Muriel laughed. "You mean those war clubs made out of poison sumac that gave us rashes so bad we missed a week of school? And my left eye actually swelled shut?"

"It was worth it though, wasn't it?"

"Yeah." Muriel smiled, and squeezed Rosalind's shoulder. "Worth every minute of itchy torture. And time with you. Though I remember Dad refused to come near us, afraid we were contagious."

Rosalind asked, "Do you hate Dad?"

"Yeah." Muriel quirked her mouth to the side, thoughtful. "I mean, I don"t want him to die, but I hate him for being such a coward and leaving you. Us. How about you?"

"I did for a little while. Now, thinking of him just makes me sad. But he lent me his dreams of building beautiful things, so I don't want to waste time hating him anymore."

On the next trip abroad, Murzie met Dylan. He was wanderlust personified, with striking eyes of green sea glass, a disarming smile, and an unfortunate love for the 80s band Styx. By the end of what became a shared trip through Torres del Paine National Park, Murzie knew she was in deep.

Finally, Aersea wriggled free of Rosalind"s creative grasp. She was still able to effect small changes—sweeten a mug of cloudberry wine, darken the feathers of a *jordmow* in flight, change the shape of a distant stratocumulus cloud—but she was no longer the architect of Aersea.

She often felt her life had become an exercise in settling for less—less magic, less running, fewer breaths. *No,* she'd tell herself. *Not settling for less, but embracing what remains.*

The next postcard read:

> *Hiking the Torres del Paine Circuit. Rained all day. You (Energizer) and I got drenched, but Gray Glacier is amazing. I love you more than the height of Cerro San Valentín! PS: I think I've met someone.* ♥
> *Murzie*

And so Rosalind traveled, too, ranging across Aersea, a pilgrim in rough clothing trying to squeeze what she could out of every minute she had left. What she'd loved about running, she poured into hiking and exploring Aersea. She studied the electric-blue icebergs that slid along the surface of *Tarn Screar*, and immersed herself in their blissful silence. Wandering among the massive cloudwoods of *Gruluth*

Mons, she wove garlands of their arm length pine needles. She explored the *Gor Sezu* foothills, and passed between the jagged *Hasaped Loam* mountains.

And then, when Rosalind thought she must be somewhere in her late twenties in Aersea years, she also met someone. Heliotrope was a blacksmith with an incongruous, delicate name. Hels, as she preferred to be called, was most certainly not fragile. She was forge-baked and had the low deep laugh of a bellows. When Rosalind was in her strong arms, she nearly forgot about home and her dying body. Rosalind learned Vobidian, the language of the southern *Farth Girchead* peninsula, and the most commonly spoken tongue of Aersea, while Hels picked up a bit of English.

Back at home, a postcard from Portugal read:

> *Took a wine tour in the Baixa Corgo of the Douro River. Forgot sunscreen. Terribly sunburned. But you (Energizer) and I got buzzed on vinho verde, so the pain is minimal. I love you more than the number of bridges in Porto! Dylan says hello.* ♥ *Murzie*

Muriel found Rosalind more and more detached with every visit, and her health in exponential decline. She began to wonder how Rosalind could possibly still be alive in her wasted body. Muriel hesitated to tell Rosalind about Dylan's proposing atop one of the towers of Kinnitty Castle under an Irish sunset.

"I'm super happy...for you," Rosalind said, wishing that she'd be there for the wedding, but knowing she wouldn't be alive that long.

"I love you, Rosie. You're the best little sister I could have possibly asked for." Muriel never missed an opportunity to tell Rosalind she loved her, because she never knew when it might be the last time.

In Aersea, Rosalind poured every last bit of her creation magic into two items: a small cloudstone sculpture of intertwined flowers—a rose and a cluster of heliotrope. And a key that she hoped would do what she asked it to do.

Hels asked, "Where do you disappear to, when you leave me?"

Because when Rosalind woke in the real world, she disappeared from Aersea. How do you tell your lover that you're from another world, and that your body is dying? The tears spilled out of Rosalind. "I want you to know how much your love has meant to me. I never expected such a gift in the short time I had." It felt unfair to Rosalind: she had not one, but two worlds to lose.

"You make it sound like you're dying," Hels said, fear in her voice.

"I had a life before you. And I fear that life will soon take me away." Rosalind handed her a small package wrapped in white linen.

Hels gave a small laugh and handed Rosalind a delicate and intricate pounded copper box in return. Hels said, "Looks like you're not the only one giving gifts." When Rosalind lifted the box's cover, she found a fine silver mirror in the felt-lined interior. In the mirror, she thought she caught a flash of Murzie, Dylan, and Energizer, looking out over a serpentine river edged with small, terracotta roofed houses. The image disappeared quickly enough that Rosalind thought she'd imagined it.

Then Hels unwrapped her present to reveal the cloudstone sculpture of intertwined flowers. Rosalind said, "And I also want you to have this," handing Hels the well-loved and well-used ball-peen hammer that Rosalind's father had given to her. Or at least the version she'd created to design Aersea. Was it only a facsimile? When was the last time she'd seen that hammer in the real world?

The next morning, Hels woke to an empty bed, while Rosalind woke in her gaunt and skeletal body.

Muriel was there and heard Rosalind mutter, "ꔷ꘎ ꕉ꘎ꕉ ꖤ꘎ꕉꕤ꘎꘎."

Muriel asked, "What was that?" Muriel knew words in a dozen languages, and could at least recognize a dozen more languages. And this was nothing she'd heard.

Rosalind drew in a ragged breath and said, "I think ... I said ... I love you, ... in Vobidian ... language of Aersea." Muriel then knew that Rosalind was probably measuring her life in days, and maybe less. Rosalind's words hadn't sounded like gibberish, but couldn't have been anything else. Muriel was now with her constantly, afraid to leave her bedside.

The next morning, Rosalind managed to force a whisper out: "... love you ... Murzie ... you're ... best ... big sister ... I could have."

"I love you, too, kiddo. Please don't leave me." But Rosalind didn't respond, lapsing into an unmoving silence—her breath shallow, her heartbeat slowing, slowing, slowing.

Then Rosalind took her last breath on Earth—

Muriel held onto Rosalind's hand until it went cool. She'd cried herself dry—her eyes felt raw and her head ached. Finally, she stood, and then she caught a glint of silver and white in Rosalind's left hand. She was certain it hadn't been there before. How had she missed it? Leaning over, she opened Rosalind's fingers to find a white stone skeleton key with a ball-peen hammer emblazoned on the shank. It was so light it practically floated on her open palm.

—and then Rosalind, just one moment later, took her first true breath in Aersea, opening her eyes to see Hels, a worried expression on her face.

A postcard rested in Hel's hands.

> *You (Energizer) and I are leaving on the first plane out of Kalispell tomorrow. I'll probably beat this postcard back, but can't wait to see you. Love you to Aersea and back!* ♥
> *Murzie*

As Muriel approached the bathroom sink, she couldn't imagine how she'd live in a world without Rosalind. She splashed water on her face and looked at herself in the mirror. She looked terrible. But then, for just a moment, Rosalind's face flickered in the reflection. The mirror shimmered like mercury and a small keyhole appeared on its surface. Muriel hesitated, wondering if any of this was real. Could all of those things that Rosalind had told Muriel about Aersea be true? Maybe this was a portal to oblivion—Rosalind had died. Would Murzie be joining her? And if she left, what about Dylan? Pulling Rosalind's cloudstone key from her pocket, Muriel weighed it in her palm. Looking up at the keyhole, she saw that it was smaller. Almost imperceptibly, it was shrinking—there was a diminishing window of time to decide.

Muriel lived a whole life in a few stretched out moments—she married Dylan, they bought a tiny blue bungalow to live in. They got a little pup, a Portuguese podengo pequeno they named Azores. Then they had two daughters, Harper and Isla, born a few years apart. They wrote, they traveled. They loved.

Though Muriel thought she'd cried herself dry, a tear slid down her cheek as a single sob was pulled from her. Then she took two deep breaths, three. Back in Rosalind's bedroom, in one of her desk drawers, Muriel found an envelope and wrote Dylan's name on it. Slipping the engagement ring from her finger, she put it in the envelope and put the envelope on Rosalind's nightstand. She kissed Rosalind on the forehead. "I love you to Aersea and back, Rosie."

Standing before the mirror again, Muriel took out her phone. She stopped herself before she scrolled through pictures she and Dylan shared and instead she opened her messaging app. Tapping on Dylan's name, she typed:

> *If you truly love me, Dylan, you won't come looking for me. I know it sounds far too crazy to be true, but I've gone to Aersea.*
>
> ♥ *Murzie*

She hit send.

Setting down her cell phone, she put her hands on the edge of the sink to steady her trembling hands. Closing her eyes, she pictured Rosalind in Aersea.

Then, opening her eyes and reaching forward, Muriel slid the key into the mirror's keyhole.

See Travis Burnham's story "Rosalind Dreams of Aersea" online at Metaphorosis.
If you liked it, leave a comment. Authors love that!
Remember to subscribe to our e-mail updates so you'll know when new stories are posted.

About the story

I wrote "Rosalind Dreams of Aersea" to a prompt about building worlds, but the true heart of the story is from my own dream that our lost friends are out there somewhere in the universe. And at some point I'll meet up with them again, maybe in a fantastical world of their own design. There are personal memories of my own lost friends scattered throughout the text, so the story is also something of a home for them. I'll leave it up to readers to find those memories or maybe create their own.

A question for the author

Q: What distracts you?

A: Beauty. Travel. Prose. That's the short list (that isn't the obvious ones of baby animal videos, stress, artistic Instagram reels, and video games). As an international teacher, I'm extraordinarily lucky that I can indulge my love of travel and beauty on a daily basis. Where I'm living now, Montenegro, is chockablock with stunning views. As for the final "distraction"? By staving off the obvious, true distractions mentioned above, I can write. I have a ritual I try to follow when it comes to my final love: early morning, ocean sounds played on my headphones, a timer to keep me on track, sometimes a word-count goal, and a turned off internet. But life is really just a series of distractions and it's up to us to choose the distractions that matter.

About the author

Travis Burnham is a speculative fiction writer and science teacher. Originally from New England, he's lived in Japan, Colombia, Portugal, Malta, and the Mariana Islands, and currently teaches science at an international school in Montenegro. He's a bit of a thrill seeker, having bungee jumped in New Zealand, hiked portions of the Great Wall of China, and gone scuba diving in Bali. He's got some novels looking for homes and can be found online at travisburnham.blogspot.com.

Saving the Whales

C.J. Erick

Niemi misses the whales.

She misses the bowhead, the fin, and the southern right. She misses the grand blue, the understated minke, and the elegant sei. She misses the way water bulged like candy glass over their backs when they rose to the surface, and how it broke into liquid shards. She misses the billowing rainbows of their exhalations on cold mornings, and the percussion cannons of their tails when they announced their preposterously powerful dives-to-be.

She didn't always miss the whales. Once, she watched them, idolizing them, yearning to be with them grokking the water and not rocking in her rowboat or rolling in her Zodiac.

It is hard now, to crinkle her eyes at the sun setting on the washboard Pacific, the delicious smells of crusty sea salt and delicately rotting seaweed in her nose, the shoosh of waves not in her ears, but somehow over and around and through her, feeling the voids where the whales should be.

Her first summer post-junior year, she spent wet through her suit and behind her ears. She spent hours leaning over the side of the inflatable with an aluminum pole like a lightning rod, plunging it into the galvanic water. Algae-laden, the water was tarnished green, like corroded bronze.

At the end of the rod was magic, a flashy new hydrophone — analog, since this was 1975 — hard-wired to a plastic-wrapped tape recorder the size of a suitcase large enough to hold her entire wardrobe of jeans, tees, tanks, hair clips, and caps, and the three Lycra one-piece swimsuits she rotated throughout the summer. Behind her, the annoying drum of San Diego, a million miles from the farm in Illinois, interfered with the recording.

She couldn't hear the sounds they were recording. She and her research partner, Floyd, whom she'd picked because he was gay and she could trust him not to use her exuberance like a date-rape drug as one professor had tried to. The voices of the grays were well below human hearing, but she'd manipulated them through the miracle of mid-Seventies sound manipulation, applied in the biology department's sound room. Now their eerie songs, replayed through the stereo speakers, touched something primal within her, like a deep siren call, the come-hither seduction of sensuous clicks and thrums and moans exotic and otherworldly.

Her senses, once piqued, would never rest.

Whales went missing.

First, the pods of minkes that frequented the central Pacific failed to arrive that year. Biologists blamed it on the failure of the last major shelf of Antarctic ice, a diversion in the ocean currents, red tides, overfishing, and even sunspots.

Niemi knew better. But her suspicions were confirmed through a chance encounter. She'd been following a small pod of the slender gray creatures at a distance, quietly rowing after them, letting the airfoil sail of her little sun-bleached white sailboat push her along as much as possible.

Lights appeared in the sky. Two silent machines the color and size and shape of pre-World-War dirigibles lowered as one imagined the carcass of a whale might fall into the lightless deep. The craft settled into the waves, kilometers from shore, well away from the sight of land. Great doors opened in the vessels' ends, and whales swam into them two by two. And then the great craft closed their doors and lifted steadily into the sky, their lights extinguished, until they grew as small as sailing ships curving away over the horizon, and disappeared.

Niemi had watched, asking herself why these ships were taking the whales, and why the whales were boarding without a struggle.

In the weeks that followed, she contacted every agency she thought would have interest in her sightings, in the disappearances. But what agency would have the authority to investigate? The California State Police? After three calls and visit to the headquarters in San Diego County, they refused to speak to her. The CIA? Probably weather balloons, was all they offered, and dismissed her. A young biologist from NOAA, the National Oceanographic and Atmospheric Administration, met with her briefly, but tried to push her observations toward illegal whaling operations, probably by Chinese fishing companies, which were suffering as ocean stocks of fish collapsed further from the unrecoverable levels in the 2020s.

Lights in the sky. Alien visitors harvesting the world's cetaceans? No one would believe her.

She lived on the ocean, helped conduct whales counts. She pursued a degree in marine biology, cetacean focus, and manhandled her way through a Ph.D. The degree and her well-taken thesis on cetacean language led to grants, and the grants led to the books published, the ones that sold at last after so many rejections and failures to launch: *Living with Earth's Smartest Beings* and *Love and Sex Among Krill and Plankton*. She became a name then, cited in oceanographic journals and doomed environmental legislation. But the writing wasn't about credibility or notoriety; it was about money, the money she needed, and there were many things she needed.

The world turns on coinage. She turned hers into a submersible, a truck-sized, two-person submarine. Electric. Quiet. Loaded with sensing equipment that beat most space missions.

She called it Grayfin.

Her mother died, the woman she most loved, but feared as the one most likely to lead her back to 'a practical career, Niemi'. And then seven months later her broken-hearted father passed as well, a man she'd never liked, but in whom she'd found a kinship in their complex, seldom-spoken feelings for her mother and each other.

Her brother and sisters divided the estate among themselves, leaving her out, since she was obviously more well-off than they were, though they knew nothing of sleeping on a wave-soaked dock, or spending one's own money on teaching supplies, those costs even a prestigious West Coast university passed on to untenured professors.

But seven years after she had seen the lift of the minke, had seen the lights dropping to the ocean again and again, she had her machine, her mechanical stalking whale, her way to find out why.

The sky ship, dull gray and oblong, dropped like a deflating helium balloon from the tortured sky toward the open waters of the Pacific. Silent, even several hundred miles from Baja where no one was going to hear it. It descended slightly butt-heavy, angled like Grayfin powering across the surface at full throttle, which was about to happen. Timing; timing.

The whales were out there — five hundred meters by the radar, lolling and spouting vapor in the waves. Four big blues, three females and one male. No calves, despite it being birthing season, which was sad and one explanation for all this.

Niemi's hands felt numb and twitchy on the controls.

The alien vessel leveled out and settled into the water. A white wave spread outward from the hull. After a few eternally long minutes, a vast door opened in the end facing the whales, like the mouth of an earthworm about to consume a bit of cornmeal sprinkled into its bait container.

The whales circled and then lined up two by two and swam toward the craft, but still a good two hundred meters from it. Niemi waited.

The first two spouted mightily, as if kicking the dust from their sandals, and entered the maw of the ship. As the second pair moved within a hundred meters, Niemi grasped the control handles and willed her sub to life.

She was thrown back into the seat as the nose came up. Four-thousand electric horses leaped ahead. Past the side-view screens flowed dirty green water, plastic junk, rust-colored debris, and the broken skeletons of maritime equipment. Her machine was stealthy quiet, but still the whine of the motors was in her ears like Triassic hornets. The rangefinder counted down the numbers. Four hundred meters. Three. One fifty.

The vessel's door closed, and the ship lifted from the waves, streamers of water falling from its sides like dishwater from an aluminum urn. It lifted into the sky just like the first two she'd observed, shrinking slowly, sailing over the horizon of the darkening sky.

"No!" She heard the ragged rage in her voice, the childlike cry of frustration and abandonment.

And then the light paused, descended, grew. The gray craft, now charcoal in the late twilight, touched the water, and the great doors opened again. It stood in the water, motionless, as if anchored by rigid pilings to the ocean floor two thousand feet below.

She eased her submarine forward, passing into the black mouth of the ship, watching the stars covered by a sky-colored sheet. The doors closed behind her ship, and all was dark. She could barely breathe.

She assumed they lifted into the sky, although she couldn't tell because there was no sense of motion, no acceleration, no feeling of changing momentum. She struggled to find a term for the beings who had taken her into their ship. Calling them 'extraterrestrial' would be Earth-centric, as if her planet were the center of the universe of intelligent species, when in fact the very existence of these beings and their ships proved otherwise. 'Space travelers' would imply they'd come from the endless void out beyond the wispy extremes of the atmosphere, when she had no idea where they'd come from, and almost certainly they'd not come from the void itself. And 'aliens' wasn't just human-centric but also politically disrespectful, since humans were at least as alien to these beings as the other way around.

So she settled for the Visitors, which seemed to cover just about anything nonhuman.

They allowed her to rock in the hull of the ship in complete darkness. She began to wonder if they expected her to navigate by sonar. She remembered her sonar then, and, risking offense, pinged around her ship, finding it rolling gently in the center of a large tank with featureless walls, shaped like two bathtubs stacked one upside down over the other. Two whale tails disappeared from the far end of the tank, rising upwards through a porthole into another chamber above her, apparently. Once they were through, dull blue lights came on and another door opened in the ceiling above her. Her submersible eased through it with no action on her part, rising into a smaller, egg-shaped chamber where metal rods protruded from the walls like fingers pushing through a balloon, cradling her ship gently as if holding a shiny black pouch of stingray eggs. Water drained from the chamber in seconds.

"Join us," said a voice. It was female, brash and harsh, brassy like someone speaking from a conch shell. A voice she disliked when she heard it in taped interviews; her own voice.

The main hatchway of the sub slid into its recess with a barely audible hum. The air that flowed in through the open door held all the taste and smell of boiled water. A metal walkway pushed out from the wall and stuck to the ship just below the port, dull like aluminum, soft like plastic as she walked along it step by step.

Beyond the doorway was a small chamber, surrounded on all sides and the top by clear glass, the walls of water tanks all around. A woman stood with her back to Niemi, and she knew it would be herself, even before the hologram or whatever it was turned to gaze at her over its shoulder, assessing her so closely and with such human intensity and expression that she couldn't convince herself the image wasn't real. She fought back the urge to touch it.

"You believe they are beautiful," said the woman. Beyond her, the four blue whales floated in an infinite pool, rising slowly to breathe, then sinking slowly under the surface. The otherwise colorless water was foggy brown with krill, and occasionally one of the whales would open its great beak-like mouth to allow the rich water to fill it.

"I do." She was overwhelmed as always by the beauty of the whales. The impending loss struck her like a migraine, twisting at the bones in her forehead. "Why — ?"

"All of us are different, and yet we are the same."

The woman explained that consciousness existed beyond the physical boundaries of the brain and of the body, and that all touched each other. When the predominant beings of a world

— she didn't use the word 'planet', as that excluded many places where rational beings lived — were able to harmonize, a stable tranquility could bloom, one that could last for thousands of years.

"These beings," said the Other Niemi, "they are special. They have a gift and a yearning for harmony which we've never seen before. Such a shame you humans don't recognize this, and you harm them."

"Some of us cherish them," said Niemi.

The Visitor said, "We have observed and, at times, sought to promote harmony on Earth, as is our calling. But despite these efforts, humans have not harmonized with your world, with the other rational beings there, such as the primates, the cephalopods, the avians, and of course, the whales."

Niemi said, "But we do achieve harmony — sometimes. We organize. We achieve great things. We help each other during crises and natural disaster. We even harmonize in song, just as the whales do."

"Truth. But political and resource organization is a sad caricature of the true, deep connection of a harmonized world.

"Your race has been given enough time. And these beautiful beings are needed elsewhere."

"Where? Why?" asked Niemi.

"Every world seeks harmony. These beings can help. And they deserve better."

The woman told Niemi they were telling her this because she was one of the few who listened — sometimes. If there was hope, it lay with her or others like her.

"Are you taking all the whales?" she asked.

"They speak across entire oceans," said the Other Niemi, shaking her head, perhaps preoccupied as she was with the whale's beauty. "No, we will only save the ones who wish to go. The orcas and some dolphin species have chosen to stay. Their food supplies are doing well for now, and they like interacting with humans. We will come back for them if they call."

"Will you bring the other whales back, once their work is done?"

"No."

Niemi paused, frozen by an aching she couldn't explain or readily locate.

"May I go with them?"

"No."

Nothing else. No explanation, no conditions. Just no.

Niemi wasn't allowed to protest or plead or fall to her knees and beg. One minute she was standing talking to this Other Niemi, or a diagram that looked and sounded exactly like video and audio of her, and the next she awoke in her submersible, washing back and forth in two-meter waves in the open sea. The ship and the whales were gone.

She sat and rocked and wept for as long as it took.

Niemi convinced a department head to support her for another grant, and she used it to finance expeditions to record whale song, and computer time to translate. She followed the herds, playing their own recorded voices to them. She paid for seeding of plankton and devised outriggers for Grayfin to scoop waste from the bleary seawater, and when that didn't make a dent in the floating and sinking trash, she had automobile-sized drone submarines built, rigged with nets to catch trash. But they did little except tangle with fish and turtles and jellyfish. The entropy of waste was pervasive and resistant.

Whale sightings and counts continued to dwindle, pointing to cataclysmic losses. Scientists and politicians and fishermen argued not over the why, but over whether this was a good or bad thing, since whales were known to reduce fishing trawler yields, and feeding the world was hard, so hard, so bloody hard to make profitable.

She spent much of her time following the orca pods, continuing to journal and sketch individuals, just as she'd done since her first whale watching excursion as a young teen on a school trip, the prize for winning a climate science award. Now, she had Grayfin, where she lived most days.

One day, she languished like an empty water bottle in calm waters well off San Diego, where one couldn't see the land and where few boats ventured. She was there because bright lights in the sky had been reported for several nights over the previous month. She turned the sound system off, the sonar sensors, the radar, the infrared thermographs, the radio.

Was it harmony she felt then, alone, like a dead piece of kelp being nibbled by tiny crabs? The harmony of the carcass of a sei whale stinking the water with the promise of food and habitat for months, before sinking into the lightless depths to provide fodder and shelter for blind eels and tube worms and beaked fish that would never see a rainbow? Or was it just loneliness, alienation?

Her eyes were to the sky, and she didn't notice them until they were nearly upon her, black and white looping shapes in the water, a dozen or more, bulky cetacean missiles, moving silently as one body, as only beings who knew each other well could. She didn't move as the pod of orcas approached and circled her. She kept the hydrophones off to avoid spooking the pod, but their clicks and whistles resonated through the craft's thin titanium shell.

They flowed around her in an intricate swirl of day-and-night bodies, then away into a funnel, leaving her. She was drawn to them as into a whirlpool. She touched the controls and followed across open water, following their bulging rhythms and infrequent breaths, to where she didn't know, and suddenly didn't care, but when they arrived it was obvious why. An old container ship, sunk so that its deck lay just above the surface, flat and open like an ice floe. It wasn't on any maps she knew of, but sonar showed it anchored to the bottom by strands of fishing net and cable, probably communication cables mistakenly dredged up, spelling its doom.

On the ship were dozens of sea lions, letting the afternoon sun broil their skin to a fearsome pink, like monsters from some children's anime film. Niemi breached Grayfin a hundred yards away, and climbed out to watch, a small hand-held camera ready.

Three of the orcas stormed the ship's deck, landing on their bellies with only their tails in the water, each grasping a mature sea lion in its mouth, wiggling their water-wet bodies back into the water, shaking the lions and dragging them down through the broken pane of the ocean's surface, down into clouds of red, before disappearing out of sight. The lions scrambling on the deck roared and retreated to the center of the ship, crushing smaller females, pushing others off into the water, where some didn't make it back to the safety of the ship's deck before being sucked down by domino torpedoes.

She knew she should record this event, but she lacked the strength to raise and point the camera. For whom would she take the pictures? For whom capture it on video? For some vulgar wildlife reality show, another outlet for those who enjoyed the violence of nature, never seeing the necessity or reason for it?

Niemi lost track of time watching the orcas circle the ship. The lions crowded together in a wary crush of gray-pink bodies. Niemi was wondering what she should do next, knowing it was already too late to return to the harbor before night and not caring much about that either.

A single orca approached, a large female, with clean lines as if painted, her shorter female's dorsal fin curving at the end, and a gray marking shaped like a human hand at the end of her left pectoral fin. Niemi remembered this whale woman, a mother she'd followed for three breeding seasons, one who'd raised three calves with brutal efficiency and care. She'd named the woman Mileva, for reasons she couldn't remember.

Mileva swam to Niemi's vessel and spit a melon-sized chunk of sea lion flesh onto the sun-beaten hull of the sub, like a grill chef dropping a slab of cod onto an aluminum fry pan. It sizzled.

Mileva rocked her face in the waves, blowing breath expectantly. Niemi eyed the fatty mass and gray hide on the hull, and her stomach grumbled.

Mileva whistled and blew a geyser of hot vapor toward Niemi, showering her in acrid spit.

Niemi scooted to the edge of the sub, scooped up the flesh, and sat holding it, feeling her throat tighten at the glowing, shiny meat, which seemed to pulse in her hands.

She bit, chewed the jelly-like flesh, tasted blood and rank oil and noxious umami; gagged and swallowed.

She swallowed another bite. She vomited into the water. She bit again, swallowed. Vomited. Her head rocked, vision blackening. She fell to her side on the hull, unable to rise.

The orca eased alongside her sub, its black eye almost invisible against its ebon skin, the large white patch above it like the luminous white eye of a phantom. The whale's gray saddle patch curved about her back like a knitted sweater. It turned, swirling, and lifted a flipper and swept it away from the craft, the gray hand patch at its tip beckoning.

Niemi thought about her snorkel gear, donning the wet suit over her thin cotton shirt and shorts, and the flippers, but instead let her body slide from the sub's hull into the cold water. Immediately her nausea passed, and she bobbed easily in the infinite soup of ocean, her clothing clinging to her like tissue paper. Mileva's head bobbed in the light waves. Was this a nod? The great black and white being slid away like a ghost, her flipper rising once to beckon again. Other orca had gathered at a distance, blowing steam, whistling, pulsations of sound tapping at Niemi's skin.

Mileva, now twenty yards from the ship, whistled loudly.

Niemi pushed away, settling into an easy swim — she could swim for hours without tiring, so much time spent in the water. But it was cold, and she was thin and would chill quickly in the Pacific water.

She came within ten feet of the huge woman whale. Mileva stroked her tail to ease away. Leading her away.

Niemi swam. Her submersible Grayfin fell away behind her.

Mileva played this game several times, letting Niemi approach, then pulling away. Cat and mouse? The other whales swam with them, to each side, remaining yards away, like spectators at a long-distance race, following the runners.

Then, after a hard, muscular thrust of tail, Mileva dove and surfaced facing Niemi, blocking her path, just ten feet in front. She waited.

Niemi paused, then swam toward the whale woman. She was at the whale's mercy, hundreds of yards from Grayfin, more vulnerable than the sea lions Mileva's pod had attacked earlier. She stopped just outside touching reach of the whale's black and white snout, which bobbed like a marker buoy, shiny as rubberized paint. The whistling of the other whales stopped. There was only the sound of the ocean around them; the susurrus of the waves, the clicks of sea creatures, the bellowing of the sea lions on the rogue ship, the screes of gulls and shearwaters scavenging the remains or hunting the small fish drawn to the blood.

Mileva swam to the side, around Niem. She turned, opened her mouth, and gripped Niemi by the chest. Teeth dug into

Niemi's skin in a hundred places. She closed her eyes.

Mileva held her in her mouth, pulled her, brushed her stomach with her great sandpaper tongue. Niemi fought the urge to push the whale away, to throw a fist at Mileva's eye. Mileva raised her partly from the water, swam in a circle, as if showing this prize to the others.

Then she opened her mouth and released Niemi. She swam ten feet away and waited, lolling in the waves, once again a dark phantom with ghostly patches.

Niemi felt the sting of seawater on small cuts on her side, her arm, her belly. She could breathe, but she wanted to vomit again.

What did the whale want from her now? It lay expectantly in the water, waiting. She could swim back for her sub, if the currents weren't taking it away from her, beyond her reach. But that would be returning to who she had been before this night, this act of connection from Mileva. That's what it was, surely. The whale could have killed her, but hadn't. The pod could have ignored her and swum away, but remained, the others again swimming in a circle around her and Mileva, whistling, blowing breath.

They were asking "Are you one of us?"

Niemi leaned forward, stroked the water with her cold arms, feeling the stings, the chill, the touch of microscopic stingers from tiny krill and squid, how her skin loved the water, the caress as it passed over her arms, her shoulders, her back.

She reached Mileva in a dozen strong strokes. She gripped the flipper nearest her, the one with the shape of a gray human hand. She gripped the end of the flipper in her teeth, held it there, pulled.

Mileva's small black eye, two feet away from hers, studied her.

She held the flipper in her teeth as long as Mileva had held her body, then released and kicked away. She placed two fingers in her mouth and blew air, spitting water, phlegm, giving a harsh rasping whine at first, and then a loud clear whistle, which cut the air and breeze, silencing the birds and the other whales.

Mileva nodded, whistled back.

She swam to Niemi, leaned over to allow the woman to grip her dorsal fin. With Niemi clinging, Mileva snapped her tail, suddenly a whistling steam ship plowing the waves. She covered the quarter mile to Grayfin in a few moments, Niemi holding tight with both hands.

At the sub, Niemi, suddenly very tired, eased back into the water, swam to the boarding ladder, climbed onto the sub's hull and knelt there, too tired to stand. Mileva, head pointing straight up, spun twice like a great black and white top, then swam away, pausing once to turn back, before disappearing beneath the dancing moonlit surface, leaving hardly a ripple in her wake.

They should, all creatures, leave the world that way, with barely a ripple marking their passage.

The next two times Niemi met Mileva and the whales, she ate of what she was offered, sea lion meat, or seal, or chunks of raw tuna or shark, she vomited. After that, she didn't vomit again.

Two calves were born, in one of the new 'conservation' sea parks, "Whales Forever," just south of San Diego, from one orca female, twins, an almost impossible miracle. A sign, many pro-captivity lobbyists said, that their programs were needed and helpful. The foundation would preserve the remaining whales through reproduction and nurturing programs, funded by interactive aquariums, agility and skills displays, swimming with the whales events.

It was harmony, of a sort, with the underlying dark shadow of corporate profit driving the enterprise.

Niemi was running a monthly educational program at middle schools, along the West Coast of the US and into Canada usually, but sometimes invited to progressive districts near Chicago, New England, even Austin and Minneapolis. Her theme was simple — "Whales are People." She was loved or hated, invited or banned. And always, always threatened. For her own protection, she became a licensed firearm carrier, and hated the need.

At the news of the miracle birth, she paused her program, spending more time on the water, her Eden, the garden she'd been pulled away from too often as she taught and wrote. Even she had bills to pay, and the grants came less often. She was too controversial.

Miracle calves, young whale children who would be raised wrong, never learn what they needed to survive in the sea, never know the true joy of pod life.

Never learn to kill for food and survival.

She requested a meeting with the sea park administrators, on the premise of being allowed to produce multi-media works for promotion of the twins, watch their lives grow. It would be like an orca version of the Hollywood film *Truman*, lives lived in a virtual-sea. A morning swim and simulated hunting. Whistling conversations with the head keeper, other staff, and virtual pod-mates. Games and entertainment with their mother and the other aquatic residents. Fun for all. And all the funding they'd need for the next ten years.

Her work was known then, over a dozen books, webinars, sea-cliff retreats for the well-heeled. She wasn't despised as much as she would be, not yet labeled an 'ultra-libertard', an 'ocean-head', a 'whale groomer'. The foundation accepted her request.

The offices where they met were located on the harbor. The ground floor conference room in the white-pillared mausoleum-like box was all windows on one wall, with a clear view of the newly-built aquarium sitting near the water, like a silver domed cosmetic box pushed there by some great hand and left to face the surf. It was a white concrete monument, not a home for sentient beings. Yet these people thought they understood cetaceans.

She'd come alone. They'd brought video-documentarians, local politicians, corporate sponsors.

After introductions, she listened through two hours of effusive promotional ideas, their vision of a grand cooperative union between human and orca, an experiment in sustainable harmony, cooperation, and mutual benefit. After this, as her patient silence endured, their enthusiasm flagged, their voices one by one fell quiet. The room's attention shifted unconsciously to the foundation's director, Mrs. Delilah Fernace, founder and CEO of God's True Foods, an organic testing and services corporation, a woman who Neimi might have liked, had she not been so much the aggressive charitable type, for whom altruism was just another arena.

At the end of the presentations, Mrs. Fernace asked Niemi, "What do you think?"

To which, Niemi said simply "It's been tried."

"But not like we intend. This isn't just a sea-zoo we're planning. This is to be a real, working environment. Humans will not make all the decisions. The orcas and dolphins here will be voting members. And we'd like you to show us to hear their voices."

A pang of earnestness struck Niemi, and she almost fell for the spell. Mrs. Fernace was a gifted visionary. One wanted to believe in anything she set forth.

"As long as there are walls," said Niemi, "this will be not a zoo, not a 'zoological garden'. It will be a prison. And the whales will not speak truly. You have been blessed with a miracle birth of fully-sentient beings. You must let them go. Back to the sea, now, while they can still adapt. If you don't act now, they will die. Perhaps not physically, but emotionally. They will not live as they would wish."

Mrs. Fernace sat silently for a moment, her face reddening.

She said, at last, "We respected you and offered you our hand in cooperation. But you've come under false pretenses, with no intention of joining us. This meeting is over."

The construction of the facility continued, larger tanks, natural plants and settings, like nothing ever built before, and the orca twins and their mother seemed well. They were allowed to interact with orcas in the wild — at least at a distance, since the wild ones stayed away. The captives grew less healthy, less vocal, eating less of the farmed fish they were given, more prone to lethargy.

Niemi was asked about these events during one of her podcasts. Her words were few. "They have heard the voices of their cousins, and they know of the true world they are missing."

Two months later and six months after the miracle birth, a summer strain of Covid virus swept through, this strain virulent among most mammals. The mother and calves were stricken, and only one calf survived. After two months of anti-viral treatments and round-the-clock care, it was a thin version of itself, alive but hardly thriving.

Niemi was asked to speak at a contentious panel discussion on ocean farming, which many felt was the only way to address food shortages among the world's eleven billion humans. Each panelist was allowed closing statements, and Niemi requested to be the last to speak. Rather than reiterate her feelings that ocean farming must be closely-controlled to prevent exploitation and environmental damage, she made a plea.

"This is to the director of 'Whales Forever'. Mrs. Fernace — give me the child. If you truly believe in God's work, give me the child, or it will not live."

Days passed, and then Niemi received a terse message from the foundation's matriarch, delivered in person by a young woman oceanographer, one who had attended several of Niemi's webinars.

The handwritten note read, "The child will be placed in your hands. My messenger, Ms. Montez, will help with the arrangements."

In Grayfin, Niemi led the foundation's vessel carrying the young orca in a watered sling. She hadn't seen Mileva's pod for weeks, but they found her within two hours of the ships leaving the San Diego harbor.

Niemi entered the water first, in scuba gear. The young orphaned orca, a beautiful female called 'Seaflower' by the institute, was lowered into the rolling waves. Niemi and Tanya Montez, the whale's main caregiver, moved with her as she slipped from the harness into the open water, eyeing Tanya wildly, and Niemi with suspicion.

The pod drifted slowly in like ghosts, quietly clicking, two young females moving closest. Fights between orca pods were rare, and strangers were generally accepted or ignored as the extreme. DNA evidence showed that orca females rarely mated within their own pods, so interactions were common, if only for biodiversity.

But there were no certainties.

Seaflower clicked and then one of the wild females whistled. The poor young stranger tried a soft whistle. And then the two females swam in a pattern before the newling, and she followed, away into the ocean gloom.

Would Seaflower tell them of her life among the humans, her illness, the loss of her mother and sister? Was their language so richly sophisticated?

Mileva appeared then, a dark slow-speed torpedo. Tanya started to retreat, but Niemi waved her fear away. The orca swam closer, passing gaze on Tanya, then paused near Niemi, before swimming away with a rocking motion, disappearing after the others. The pod's whistles and clicks grew more distant.

The following week, Tanya joined Niemi's inner circle.

Following the publicity around Seaflower's release, scientists from China and Finland contacted Niemi with a proposal they said she would find attractive. They met secretly, in an abandoned fishers' shed, with two of her assistants knocking around outside on the aged and warped pier. The researchers had a proposal, one that would have intrigued anyone who worked with the few whale species still observed in the wild.

They sat away from her, as if repelled by her natural odor. Dr. Wen Zhang allowed Dr. Hern Ruminen to speak first.

"We have a process. We can place a living human brain inside the skull of a young juvenile member of Orcinus orca."

He explained how they intended to bio-splice the nerves to the medulla oblongata, microsurgery involving elaborate medical robotics and supercomputer AI. The rest of the details bulged like a tide and bowled into Niemi, where she sat in the small office of a fish market south of the city, one of the last places in the USA where one might avoid observation. She knew what they were proposing, even without the details. She would become a whale.

"Of course, the transition," said Dr. Zhang, in a precise voice devoid of accent, "will be very similar to a new birth. Every aspect of living, breathing, swimming, eating, must be learned from the first day of life. There will be no parallel experience. No amount of empathy or living among the subject species will prepare the human participant for this irreversible process." When she didn't react, he cast a side glance at the rigid, gray-templed form of Dr. Ruminen. His voice lost some of its enthusiasm. "This is why it is necessary to place the human brain into the skull of a newborn specimen."

They knew of her writings on inter-species connection, the potential for biological harmony, the only way for the tortured modern world to survive, and then thrive. All living things were part of the same biome, the microcosm bound only by the limits of the atmosphere, and perhaps not even that.

And yet these scientists, these researchers, although sympathetic to her cause, they felt this process, this experiment, this exploitation would be attractive to her. This was the best idea they could bring to her.

"Where will you find a recipient?" she asked, without inflection. Her voice sounded brassy and alien, echoing in the small shack. She had grown to dislike speaking. She had taken to humming along with her many recordings of whale song, those wondrous voices now lost, like the songs of ancient humans.

"It will be necessary to capture a mature, pregnant female and extract a late-term fetus."

Niemi nodded. She choked back her rage, told them it was a very interesting project, and thanked them for considering her. She would respond within a few weeks.

She followed the research through spies she'd placed at their institutions. Months later, after they'd given up on her repeated postponements and found a willing participant, a young military scientist, when the capture ships were being stocked and prepared for the initial hunt, she and three assistants used guided drone submarines to attach deep sonic beacons on the ships' hulls, near the drive units. She was able to track them at all times, and so were the orcas.

Their efforts to capture a pregnant female were unsuccessful.

They came after her, of course. Not the researchers, but the others she was angering the most; international fishing corporations, whose ships were increasingly assaulted by marine life; major religious institutions, whose spiritual messages she was subverting with her drive for harmony and unity through nature, the message that humans lived within nature and not above it, that all living things were citizens, not resources; governments, whose citizens more and more refused to pay for the privilege of citizenship, who were choosing to join the growing movement to an untethered oceanic community, a community that wasn't just universally human, but for all creatures, all living things.

She and many of her followers gathered on handmade rafts and platforms, offshore from San Diego Harbor. They were harassed occasionally by military aircraft, but they were loose, able to deconstruct their floating base in minutes, allow the currents to scatter them, with the occasional help of friendly orcas.

'Humans First' movements hated her the most, and she found great satisfaction in that.

More than once, vigilantes from anti-whale groups attacked them, with weaponized drones and small helicopters. Such attacks were never surprises, always given away by internet traffic, monitored with little effort by friends of Niemi's following. By the time the drones arrived, the flotilla would have vanished, dispersed as if it had never been.

Save one vessel, a small submersible, floating among the black and white bodies and vaporous spray of orcas. If the attackers had looked closely, they would have seen that the largest orca female had a gray marking on one fin, in the shape of a human hand. When the drones fell upon them, they dove straight down, gone in seconds, beyond the reach of weapons and soon beyond the reach of air-based radar and sonar.

The attackers waited. They must rise for breath. They pursued did rise, single whales rising to breathe and dive again in dozens of locations miles apart, and Niemi's submarine was not among them.

But the orca attacks on fishing ships became more sporadic, the losses less important.

The scarcity economics that spread in every continent brought more famine, more disease, and more anger. The world was coming to war, and Niemi's pesky social experiment was forgotten for a time. It became a dim, distasteful memory to most. But to some, a legend.

Her following, hidden in ocean shadows, continued to grow. And with less food competition from other whales and sea predators, the numbers of orcas and the few dolphin species grew with her following.

On a day of gray skies, Mileva lingered by Grayfin, not venturing out, not blowing vapor well up to splash on Niemi where she ate her sea greens, not following the others as she had come to do, watching the younger ones hunt the seas and return to the old grandmother with a hunk of flesh. The time had come for her to pass on, and knowing it was coming still hadn't prepared Niemi.

Twenty-five years had passed for them together. She had loved this whale woman more than her own mother. The connection between them — this was the fabric of heaven, the hope of eternity, the bond of hand to flipper, bodies, worlds, universes.

Mileva — a Slavic name meaning 'gracious'.

Mileva's steamy breaths came slower and shallower, until they just ceased. Her body rocked against Grayfin's hull, as against a lover.

Soon, several big females came to grasp the elder mother by her fins and pull her away, to where Niemi never knew.

Niemi had not wept in many years. But with this loss, she remembered how.

The years passed, like cool ocean waters passing over the skin, leaving the sands and stings and memories of great swims.

They are thousands now, living on a floating island caravan just within sight of the coast, where lay the war-damaged cities and their damaged people. Ropes of kelp and knots of barnacles and coral cling to the old fishing nets and foam plastic balloons lashed beneath, providing ballast, stability when storms rage against it. Gardens spring from the sand and dirt they've collected, seeds and feces dropped by birds, thousands of them. Shimmering fish pinwheel in swarms around and beneath the island. The caravan moves on the wind, nudged at times by those who built cloth sails and turbine masts, holding it in favorable waters.

Guarded by orcas; guided by the moon, the stars, the sun.

It is a warm night.

Niemi climbs from the tarnished and dented and welded hull of Grayfin to gaze upon the caravan a quarter-mile away. A floating city-state it has become, nothing she ever imagined or wanted, a thing sprung from the harmony of being, the harmony of beings. She may have inspired it, but she isn't part of it, is she? Haven't they come for themselves, thinking of her as an idea only? She walks among them sometimes, the hushed tones as she passes, the orcas ever-present. The symbol of the mother orca Mileva is sown into many of their sails, with the gray, human hand pattern on her fin.

The night sky is brilliant, bisected by the pale ribbon of the Milky Way. Her sense of smell is going the way of her body, her sight, her strength, yet the sea air is alive with salt and life, and the hint of death, the ultimate certainty. There is harmony even in the smell of the sea.

How many worlds out there have lost their harmony? How many have lost their whales?

This is the ocean; a pool of interaction, living and passing on, woven lives and minerals and elements. Harmony, in a word. One cannot escape it, not without leaving most of oneself behind, in the infinite song that bounces from shore to shore, island to continent, depth to sky.

Come back, lights, bring our people back home.

The sky remains quiet, the lights do not come. They stopped coming decades ago.

Away over in the colony, flutes and horns, stringed boxes and deep drums begin to play a lilting song — not a song, really, more a feeling, a yearning, a reaching out for ears and jaw teeth to hear. Wailing, whistles, clicks of wood and stone and metal rod. Language in every form, every pitch, vibration in every frequency.

Beneath her, the orcas speak, respond to the music, join the conversation. Niemi has listened to their voices for so many years now, decades, that their language has become her own, like it was her first. She hears every sound, every idea, every dream.

They are thousands now, on hundreds of floating pods in every sea and ocean, around and near every port, the human-orca communities, in salty seas all over the planet, patrolling the shoals, monitoring the sea farming, keeping it within sustainable boundaries. There is spill-over, communities on land springing up, the harmonizing of humans with other primates, elephants, even forests, nearly doomed at one time, but sprouting back to life. The movement was now a tidal wave.

It all started with a few real believers dipping into the water, a ritual they all performed now, to leave the security and technology behind for a short time, to become one with the sea, one with the orcas, to be completely vulnerable. To have a faith like no other, the faith in the impossible community of living spirits. They didn't call it a baptism. The didn't call it anything.

The pain hits Niemi again, this time too hard to ignore, the malignancy that spread from her lungs — micro-dust sarcoma, doctors explained, a condition even bathing in the nurturing salt waters can't cure, so many afflicted with it now. If only she'd had more time to build the sky pods— communities of humans and birds, to patrol and scour. She tries to breath, but great invisible hands crush her from both sides.

"Niemi?" Tanya hears her fall, rushes from Grayfin's cabin, is there, grasping her shoulder.

"It's...huh...time, sister."

"No —"

"Yes. I need...to be...in the water."

Dark fins cut through the ocean soup in the twilight — they always know somehow, the tall black fins of the males, the shorter, sometimes curved dorsals of the females. And there among them, Seaflower, tulip-shaped patches of white on her flippers. They always know, these great beings, these wise ones of the sea. They know when one of their own is about to pass.

"Help me...get these off." Niemi struggles to unbutton the shirt and trousers, but Tanya is there to help.

Many more orca come, as Tanya helps her ease into the cool water, so nice, so delicate a caress on her skin.

"Where...are the lights?" Niemi studies the sky, knowing they are coming, coming to bring their friends, their other peoples back home. The world is better, ready for them. There is harmony now. Isn't this enough?

"What, Niemi? I can barely hear you."

No matter. She can't draw the breath to talk. The whales are around her in the water now, buoying her up, nuzzling her, holding her up to the crisp air as they would a newborn calf. Funny that the air bites her lungs so. Funny how the sky darkens. Is a storm coming?

There. Lights in the sky, moving across the stars, no satellite or abandoned space station. No, these lights are falling, growing brighter as they sink through the miles of atmosphere. Great tankers of water, carrying the children of those huge beings who left before. They are coming. She has done enough.

Her peoples are coming home.

*See C.J. Erick's story "Saving the Whales"
online at Metaphorosis.
If you liked it, leave a comment. Authors love
that!
Remember to subscribe to our e-mail updates so
you'll know when new stories are posted.*

About the story

"Saving the Whales" was a coalescing of several themes or concepts that rolled around in my head for months. The first was the idea that consciousness isn't just a network of complex chemical reactions in the brain, but is an energy field that extends beyond the physical boundaries of the skull. This field is influenced by other people around us, environmental conditions such as air quality, and other internal processes, such as our internal biome, including bacteria, viruses, and parasites. From this idea came the concept of 'harmonizing', how all living things and perhaps natural elements come together in a universal conscious community.

Another theme expressed in this story Is that of the responsibility of humans above all other creatures to lead the stewardship of the planet. Of all living things, we have the greatest power to alter, manipulate or destroy the living environment. If this is true (and it may not be actually) then we must accept the responsibility to protect and preserve. Failing this, we risk losing it all, bringing about cataclysmic upheaval and mass extinction.

The title "Saving the Whales" seems to invoke the existing lobbies to preserve the cetaceans through ending whaling, better control of pollution, and restricting fishing and naval techniques that harm them. But the title really refers to the alien visitors who step in to protect the whales when humans have failed. The visitors see the true unique value of the whales in 'harmonizing' the world's living biosphere, and move to preserve the whales so they may rise to achieve their calling. That only the 'killer whales' choose to remain among humans is symbolic, and seems very timely with the recent increase in orcas attacking small sailing craft in several places world-wide.

Also, this story started with a line of text, the melancholy first line of the story. "Niemi misses the whales." From there, my mind took off into 'what if' land.

A question for the author

Q: What was your favorite children's book?

A: Excellent question, and I had to go back to memory lane.

I'd like to mention two books. The first is *The Little Engine That Could*. I loved this book because even as a young child I was a lover of underdogs, and those who achieve great things beyond the expectations of others, by the sheer force of self-belief. The second book could be any of the early Dr. Seuss books, but I'll say *If I Ran the Circus*. I loved the zany adventure and creative acts, the bravery of doing something strange as an occupation, and, as with all of his books, the wonderful words!

About the author

C.J. Erick writes in multiple genres, publishes novels in a space fantasy series, and dabbles in poetry. He lives in Dallas area with his wife and their rescue superhero dog Saber-Girl, calls his sourdough bread starter "Ursula" (K. Le Guin), and cooks crazy-good Cajun food for a Midwest Yankee.

www.cjerickfiction.com,   facebook.com/cj.erick.9/, Instagram: cee_jay_erick

Copyright

Title information

Metaphorosis November 2023

ISSN: 2573-136X (online)
ISBN: 978-1-64076-269-5 (e-book)
ISBN: 978-1-64076-270-1 (paperback)

Copyright

Publisher

Metaphorosis
a magazine of speculative fiction

Metaphorosis Magazine is an imprint of Metaphorosis Publishing
Neskowin, OR, USA

www.metaphorosis.com

"Metaphorosis" is a registered trademark.

Discounts available

Substantial discounts are available for educational institutions, including writing workshops. Discounts are also available for quantity purchases. For details, contact Metaphorosis at metaphorosis.com/about

Metaphorosis Publishing

Metaphorosis offers beautifully written science fiction and fantasy. Our imprints include:

Metaphorosis Magazine
Plant Based Press
Verdage
Vestige

You can also find us:
Metaphorosis@writing.exchange
@Metaphorosis
www.facebook.com/metaphorosis

Help keep Metaphorosis running by supporting us at
Patreon.com/metaphorosis

See more about some of our books on the following pages.

Metaphorosis Magazine

Metaphorosis
a magazine of speculative fiction

Metaphorosis is an online speculative fiction magazine dedicated to quality writing. We publish an original story every week, along with author bios, interviews, and notes on story origins.

We also publish monthly print and e-book issues, as well as yearly Best of and Complete anthologies.

Come and see us online at magazine.Metaphorosis.com.

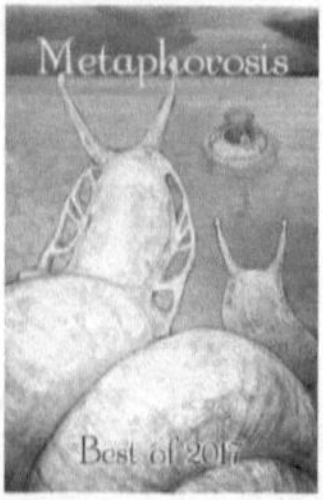

Plant Based Press

Vegan-friendly science fiction and fantasy, including anthologies of the year's best SFF stories, from 2016-2020.

Chambers of the Heart
speculative stories
by
B. Morris Allen

A heart that's a building, a dog that's a program, a woman sinking irretrievably — stories about love, loss, and motion.

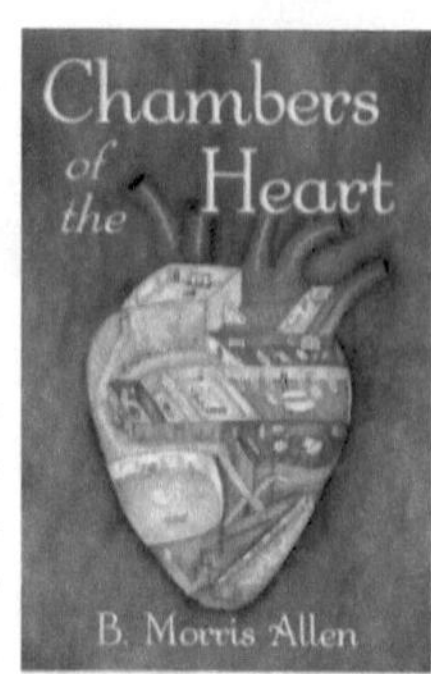

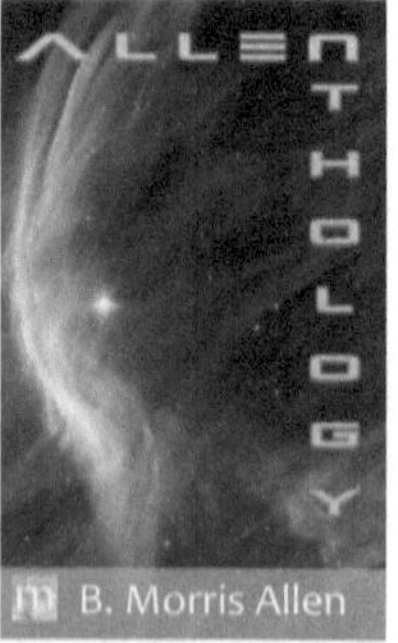

Susurrus

A darkly romantic story of magic, love, and suffering.

Allenthology: Volume I

Including three full collections of SFF stories.

Verdage

Science fiction and fantasy books for writers — full of great stories, often with an additional focus on the craft of speculative fiction writing.

Reading 5X5 x3

Changes

How do stories move from 'maybe' to published?

Here are 15 case studies of stories published in *Metaphorosis* magazine.

Reading 5X5 x2

Duets

How do authors' voices change when they collaborate?

A round-robin of five talented science fiction and fantasy authors collaborating with each other and writing solo.

Including stories by Evan Marcroft, David Gallay, J. Tynan Burke, L'Erin Ogle, and Douglas Anstruther.

Score

an SFF symphony

An anthology with an emotional score from the heights of joy to the depths of despair – but always with a little hope shining through.

Reading 5X5

Five stories, five times

See how different
writers take on
the same material.

Reading 5X5

Writers' Edition

Two extra stories,
the story seed,
and authors' notes
on writing.

Vestige

Novelettes, novellas, and novels by Metaphorosis authors.

The Nocturnals
Mariah Montoya

Night is Dangerous.
Day is deadly.

Where day and night last thirty years, humans move constantly stay ahead of the night and cruel Nocturnals that call it home. But a boy is lost out there.

Joyful Heave

Science fiction and fantasy anthologies with innovative and unusual themes.

Museum Piece
an unusual collection

A gallery of the strange and outrageous

Step right up and enter a world of wonder and oddities! These museums are not your typical tourist traps. From the Museum of Lost Dreams to the Suicide Museum, each exhibit will take you on a journey you won't soon forget.